Sweet Cowboy Kisses

Sugar Coated Cowboys: Book #2

Stephanie Berget

Cover Design: RM Duffy

Other Titles by Stephanie Berget

Change of Heart Cowboys

Radio Rose

Salt Creek Cowboys

Sugarwater Ranch

Sugar Coated Cowboys

Gimme Some Sugar

Sweet Cowboy Kisses

Cowboy's Sweetheart

DEDICATION

My Dad isn't a cowboy. In fact, the only time he's
ever been on a horse, he got thrown off on his
head, but he's one of the best men I know.
Thanks for everything, Dad.
This one's for you with love.

PROLOGUE

Kade Vaughn opened his eyes to a sea of worried faces as he lay in the dirt on the arena floor. Maybe if he focused on the pretty woman leaning over him, everything would stop spinning.

"Don't worry, Pans. I'm fine," he reassured her. At least that's what he thought he'd said. For some reason, his words got tangled up as he tried to force them out of his mouth.

"Look who's awake."

Kade squinted, trying to focus. That didn't sound like Pansy's voice.

"Kade, what state are you in?" The dark-haired woman watched him as her cool fingers held his wrist, taking his pulse.

This wasn't Pansy.

He tried to roll to his side. Needed to get up and out of the arena before Pansy saw he'd had his bell rung again. With the slight movement, the arena floor tilted like the deck of a sinking ship.

A hand on his shoulder prevented him from doing anything but sinking back into the dirt. Like he needed the help. Lying flat on his back was all he could manage.

"What state, Kade?" The voice, gentle but insistent, repeated the question as she leaned closer.

He tried for a chuckle, but it came out as more of a groan. "I'm not even sure who I am." The woman's image flickered, and he blinked slowly, twice.

She smiled, but the expression held very little humor. "Kade, how many fingers am I holding up?"

Seemed like a stupid question, but what the hell. "Four, and I'm at the college rodeo in Missoula. Did I win?" he tried to sit up, but his head—that up 'til now had hurt like a son of a bitch—spun until he thought it'd come off his shoulders. He sank back to the arena floor with a groan.

"Can you tell me what year is this?"

What was with this woman and her asinine questions? "Can't you find someone else to play Trivial Pursuit with?"

"My mother told me not to take a job dealing with cowboys. She told me I'd regret it." Grinning down at Kade, she asked, "The year?"

"Two thousand eight. Just help me up, will you?" He braced his elbows against the dirt and raised his head at least an inch and a half before a brain spasm knocked him back down.

The woman placed her hand on his shoulder. "You just lay here another minute."

When she stood, Kade could hear a murmured conversation. "Doc, are you ready for us to take him out of the arena?"

"Not yet." Apparently the woman with a thousand questions was a doctor.

The rest of the discussion drifted away as he closed his eyes and surrendered to the Van Halen drum solo pounding through his brain.

~*~

A no-nonsense voice called to Kade from beyond his stupor. "Kade, stay with me here."

When he opened his eyes, Doc Turner knelt beside him, her dark hair pulled back into a no-nonsense ponytail. Even after working for hours at the bull-riding event, her white knit shirt with the company logo was still pristine. "Hey, Doc. What's going on?"

Doctor Turner looked at least fifteen years younger

than her fifty years, but Kade had learned long ago that this woman was the best physician at Western Sports Medicine, the group that cared for injured TBC bull riders.

"Kade, where are you? What city?" The physician shifted to the side while EMTs carefully moved Kade to a stretcher.

As they strapped him down, he smiled at her. "Top Bulls and Cowboys event in Cincinnati." The fog that had shadowed his mind for the last little bit slowly lifted, and the pain in his head lessened a bit.

Doc Turner grinned. "At least you're in the right half of the country. What year is it?"

Kade snorted then stilled. It seemed his brain retaliated for the slightest movement. "2016."

"Give him the prize, gentleman. He's in the right decade." Doc shifted so he could see her better. "We're going to take you to the hospital and have them check out that hard head of yours."

"Nah, hey Doc. I'm fine. Just let me rest behind the chutes for a minute then I'll be good to go. I got all your questions right. You said so yourself."

It was Doctor Turner's turn to snort in amusement. "Not quite. We're in Nashville. Cincinnati was last week."

~*~

The ride to the hospital was uneventful, dammit. The driver refused to turn on the siren or lights, even when Kade offered him money, and the attendant didn't think his jokes were the least bit funny. The efficient staff at the hospital transferred him to a private room and had just finished doing all kinds of tests when his buddies arrived.

He'd met Chewie Diaz his first day at Montana State, and they'd hit it off like they were bull-riding clones. No food was too bad or joke too lame for the two them. Lately a kid by the name of Toby Lance had taken to following them around. Toby didn't ride too bad, did his share of driving without complaining and paid his part of the expenses, so they let him tag along.

"Good to see you're not dead." A familiar grin covered Chewie's face.

No sympathy from this bunch, and he hadn't expected any. In fact, the careful attention the nurses showed him made him kind of queasy. Made him wonder if he was really that bad off.

"You ride like a girl." Chewie punched him in the arm. "Swamp Fox must have thrown you ten feet into the air."

Kade relaxed a little. If his buddy was giving him a bad time, he was pretty sure he wasn't going to die.

"You meet any hot nurses yet?" Toby never said much, and when both men turned to their attention on him, a flush crawled up his cheeks as if he regretted speaking up now.

When Kade didn't answer, Chewie tossed a wadded up napkin at him. "You could play up the injured cowboy bit. Women like that."

"Screw you! Did I make eight?" There were some pretty nurses here, but the only thing that mattered right now was whether he'd made a qualified ride. Kade could put up with a headache for the next year if he'd finally ridden the toughest bull on the circuit.

The grins that had been on the guys faces sobered. Toby turned away, staring out the window, and Chewie's attention was suddenly focused on his boots.

"What happened?" He had to ask, but he already knew. Swamp Fox had beaten him again.

The first time he'd drawn the bull, Swamp Fox had thrown him out of the arena and into the lap of a bald, old man with a handlebar moustache. It wouldn't have been near as embarrassing if the damned bull had aimed for the drop-dead gorgeous blonde in the second row.

Add that to their match-up at the Finals last November when all he'd had to do was ride the big, yellow bull to become the TBC World Champion. He'd needed a qualified ride, any qualified ride in the tenth round to win it all. A forty-five would have done it, but Swamp Fox had spun him off at seven point nine seconds. He'd only needed one tenth of a second more for all his dreams to have come true.

Kade had poured his heart and soul into his sport for the last seven years, getting better and better. With a million dollars in prize money to the year-end World Champion, all his hard work would have paid off if he'd just been able to ride the damned bull.

Swamp Fox had stomped all over that dream.

Chewie tugged his phone out of the back pocket of his Wranglers and pulled up a video. He handed the iPhone to Kade. "Man, I thought you had him this time."

The screen on the phone was small, but the video was as clear as day. The gate cracked open and Swamp Fox's huge body rocketed high into the air with the grace of a cat. As the bull hit the ground, he slung his head to the right, trailing a long, thin line of snot.

Kade could hear the announcer. "This ain't no ordinary bull, folks. I heard tell his mama was a roller coaster and his daddy, a Tilt-A-Whirl.

He'd matched Swamp Fox move for move, shifting his hips, keeping his weight centered. Just when he began to think his buddies were giving him a hard time, and that he'd ridden the bull after all, the video showed him the truth.

With a powerful lunge, Swamp Fox threw his horns back toward his rider at the same time as Kade leaned forward to make a counter move. In the next instant, his limp body hit the dirt.

In the who's-got-the-hardest-head contest, Swamp Fox had won hands down.

The moment Kade fell from his back the big bull stopped bucking. He'd stood there, a few feet away, staring at Kade as he gave his uneven horns a slow shake. "Thought you'd ride me, huh?" he seemed to say. "Take that, amateur."

As the clowns moved in, the video ended.

Kade didn't need to see it twice. He handed the phone back to his friend. "Damn."

Chewie leaned against the wall, his fingers in his front pockets. "Man, you almost had that big bastard. If he hadn't thrown that head butt at you, you'd have ridden him for sure."

Suddenly, Kade wanted desperately to be alone. Last year, his dream had ended in the most heart-breaking way he could have imagined. Now, this year was uncertain, and he didn't want these guys to pity him. Time to change the subject.

He forced a grin as he looked at Chewie. "For a few minutes, I thought Pansy was there at the arena. I was afraid she was going to be mad as hell. That bull must have really knocked me for a loop."

Chewie looked up, finally making eye contact.

The man was one of his oldest friends, and he was the only bull-rider Kade knew who remembered Pansy Lark.

"Damn! Pansy? She would have kicked your ass for sure. I miss that girl sometimes."

No shit! So did Kade and more than sometimes.

"Who's Pansy?" Toby took another tentative attempt at joining the conversation. A long lost love was fair game, a guy could recover from that apparently, but a lost rodeo dream was too painful for the men to talk about.

"She was Kade's girlfriend in college." Chewie looked at Kade, shaking his head. "Everybody thought he was going to marry her, but the bulls got in the way. I personally think he screwed up, big time."

This subject wasn't any less painful than the last one. Kade had been thinking the same thing for a few years now. Seemed like he was always losing what he wanted most.

He opened his mouth to change the subject once again when Toby piped up. "She dumped ya, huh?"

On a good day, Toby rarely spoke more than five words. It was one of the things Kade like best about him, but it seemed he'd chosen today to mimic Gilbert Gottfried.

"Even with a concussion, I can still throw both of you out of here and not break a sweat." Kade tried to put some authority into his words, but the effort made the pounding in his head jack up.

"I'm shaking in my boots, pendejo." Chewie's laughter was cut short when a white-coated doctor came through the door, followed by Doc Turner.

Doc smiled as she shooed his friends away and swung the door closed. "Now about this head injury. I think it's time you quit riding bulls."

That was out of the question. His look must have told Doc that.

"At the very least, wear a helmet."

Kade managed to sit up straighter. He tried to shake his head, but the movement amplified the pounding in his brain. Instead, he glared at the doctors. "No and hell no. Is that clear enough?"

CHAPTER ONE

The gold beads on Pansy Lark's Cleopatra wig tapped together as she whirled to grab a dishcloth from the sink. Clouds of acrid gray smoke filled the café kitchen while the smoke alarm blasted out its migraine-generating shriek.

"Double dip damn!" After wrapping a damp dishtowel around her hand, she pulled the cupcake tins from the oven. Sliding the pans onto the granite counter, she rushed to the back door and threw it open, trying to dispel some of the concentrated, opaque smoke.

Pansy emptied the charred blobs of cake into the garbage then dropped the cupcake tins in the sink. The clatter of metal against porcelain almost masked the tinkling of the bell above the café door.

On top of burning the entire batch of tiny cakes, she had a customer.

She tossed the towel over her shoulder and pushed open the swinging door between the dining room and kitchen, only to freeze in her tracks. "Karma, you are a colossal bitch," she said under her breath.

The black haired cowboy sauntered toward the counter, an oh-so-familiar smile on his face. That smile, once upon a time, had made her heart sing. "Hey there, Sweetheart."

Now it made her heart recoil.

Seven years hadn't changed him a bit. Pressed Wranglers molded to his well-developed thighs, his T-shirt hugged his shoulder muscles, his black hair curled along his collar, just the way she'd liked it. Her first inclination was to turn tail and run, but she'd run as far as she was going to for this lifetime.

Pansy lifted her chin, and faced her worst fear—Kade Vaughn.

The cowboy slipped onto one of the red vinyl stools that ran along the counter and brightened his smile, if that was possible. Kade had the kind of grin that caused women's panties to fall off.

But not hers, not anymore.

"What's your name, honey?" Muscles worked beneath tanned skin as he leaned his forearms on the counter and gave her his undivided attention.

She remembered running her hands over those arms, the fine, dark hairs tickling her palms, his skin warm. Closing her eyes, she took a step back. She remembered too much about this cowboy.

Chancing a look into his eyes, ready to tell him to leave, she stopped. He didn't recognize her, the bastard.

To his credit—if she was forced to give him any kind of positive acknowledgement—she was about as far from the dutiful little cowgirl of her younger years as possible. And thank goodness for that.

She didn't need a stroll down a painful memory lane right now.

Seven years ago, she'd abandoned the life she'd had in Montana. She hadn't wanted to leave her horses and the thrill of running barrels, but when Kade left her and her overbearing father asked the impossible, she'd fled and not looked back.

The day her father urged her to get an abortion was too much. Leaving the things she loved behind, Pansy had changed every detail possible about herself, including her clothing, personality and possibly her thoughts. She'd become the epitome of a city girl.

"What can I get you?" She stepped farther into the room and folded her arms across her chest. She hadn't seen Kade in seven years and seeing him today was about twenty years too soon. It had taken her forever to see the man as he really was, certainly not someone she could count on. He was tumbleweed, a wanderer, who was happy to let life blow him to his next adventure.

He tilted his head as he looked at her. His eyebrows lifted as he took in the soft folds of her white dress.

She'd made this replica of the gown Liz Taylor wore in Cleopatra, and it was one of her favorites.

Then he raised his gaze to her gold trimmed black wig and overly made-up eyes.

For a moment, she thought he might see beyond the costume to who she really was. That moment was gone before she could blink.

With a slight shake of his head, he broke eye contact and grabbed a menu from the stand. "I'll have the breakfast special, eggs over easy and the bacon just this side of burnt."

A jolt of unease mixed with regret shot through her when his slate gray eyes met hers.

"Oh, and coffee. Lots of coffee."

Pansy nodded then escaped into the kitchen. Of all the small town cafes in all of the western United States, he had to walk into hers. She cracked three eggs onto the griddle beside the pile of fresh grated potatoes and four strips of bacon then dropped the shells one by one into the garbage. The loud ticking of the old school clock above the door competed with the sizzle of the food as it cooked.

Pulling a deep breath into her lungs, she let it out bit by bit. It would be okay. She didn't think Kade recognized her, at least not yet. Hopefully, their past and her pain could stay right where she'd hidden it.

Maybe he was passing through on his way to another

bull riding. If she had an ounce of luck left, he'd be gone as soon as he had breakfast. Pansy grabbed the coffee pot and a mug. Time to play up Pansy Lark, city girl, cosplayer and cook extraordinaire.

"Here you go." She poured the mug full of coffee and placed it before him. Keeping her head down, she let the locks of her wig shadow her face. "Your breakfast will be out in a minute."

"You weren't here the last time I visited East Hope." Kade's deep voice reverberated through her bones. She'd always loved his voice, and his touch, and . . .

Enough! She hurried toward the kitchen door but stopped when she reached it. It would be rude not to answer. If she hadn't been rude all those years ago, she could be polite now. "I've been here about ten months."

"Where you from? Not from around here."

"What makes you say that?" She wasn't going into her personal life. Kade had given up any right to know about her past.

"The hair-do. Don't know many East Hopians who channel Cleopatra—or any woman but a fifties country western singer." The smile he shot her way made her heart do a tap dance around her chest. "Big hair rules in these parts."

Pansy fought to keep the corners of her mouth from turning up at the visual. Big hair was indeed the norm in this small town. But she'd be damned if she'd give him the satisfaction of seeing her smile. "I like to be different." Before he could say another thing, she disappeared through the door.

She'd adopted various wigs and costumes when her life disintegrated, stepping into the personas of women who'd made their own way in the world. After she lost Maxie, she'd worked hard to become the polar opposite of the conventional small town cowgirl she'd been before, a girl who played by the rules. And she'd succeeded—until now.

Pansy slid the spatula beneath the eggs, flipping them

before turning the bacon and shredded potatoes. As she waited for the food to finish cooking, she dropped into the ancient wooden chair in the corner of the kitchen. The oak spindles on the back creaked as she settled in.

She had to get a grip. The same attraction she'd felt years ago for that damned cowboy was back and even stronger but things were different this time. She wasn't making that mistake twice.

Kade was the same footloose cowboy he'd always been, but she'd changed. The feelings she felt for him would bring her nothing but heartache. She'd finally found, if not peace then at least a measure of quietude in her life. Besides, she'd had enough heartache for three lifetimes.

The man rode bulls, and bulls were his only true love. She'd found out the hard way that nothing and no one stood in the way of Kade's desire for a world championship. Maybe he'd already won the world. Pansy didn't know. She'd made it a point to stay away from everything that had to do with rodeo.

His words from earlier jolted through her brain. *You weren't here the last time I visited East Hope.* He wasn't a stranger passing through. He knew the little town.

For peace of mind, she'd cling to the idea that he was here for a short visit, and he'd be gone soon.

After sliding the eggs onto the heavy white porcelain plate, she piled the bacon beside the hash browns. Serve the man and he'll leave the cafe. Then she'd at least have some breathing room while she figured out what to do about him.

East Hope reminded her of her hometown—their hometown. Instead of pine trees, it had sagebrush, but the people and lifestyle were the same. When she'd arrived here, she'd relaxed for the first time in years. Denver had served its purpose, getting her away from the awful memories, but it had been like living in a boarding house, not a home.

She'd considered staying in East Hope. If Kade ruined

this for her she'd never forgive him. She had come to terms with his leaving her, but she wasn't ready to let bygones be bygones. And she sure wasn't going to set herself up for another fall.

She stood and picked up the loaded plate. Time to get this over with. A glance at the big old school clock above the door told her it was time to begin preparations for the lunch crowd. Straightening her shoulders and lifting her chin, she channeled Cleo. Pansy had worked hard to become a strong woman, and she wasn't about to let a chance meeting with Kade push her back to the naïve girl she'd been.

The bell over the door announced another customer just as she entered the dining room with the food. Micah West waved to her then veered toward Kade.

Micah had married Cary, Pansy's best and only friend, the fall before, and they were expecting a baby within the next few weeks. Cary was happy, and for that, Micah had earned Pansy's loyalty.

She set the plate before Kade, smiled at Micah and turned toward the kitchen. "I'll get you some coffee, Micah."

"Wait. I'd like to introduce someone." Micah slapped Kade on the shoulder. He laid his cowboy hat top down on the counter then settled onto a stool. "This is my cousin, well, second-cousin, Kade Vaughn. He's going to be staying with us for a couple of months."

A shiver of apprehension passed through Pansy. So much for keeping her identity a secret. When he heard her name…

"Kade, this is Cary's friend, Pansy."

Kade had been looking at Micah, but now his head snapped around and his narrowed gaze burned into her. She tried to take a deep breath, but her lungs had gone on strike. He not only knew who she was, he was staying in East Hope. For several months!

Double dip dammit!

This couldn't be happening. She didn't want to leave East Hope. But the thought of being around Kade for that long made her stomach mutiny.

Both men were staring at her.

She needed to do something—respond, regain control. She needed to do it now. Pansy stuck out her hand. "Nice to meet you, Mr. Vaughn." Maybe, if Kade could keep his mouth shut, she could keep Micah and Cary in the dark about her relationship with Kade for a while longer. The less she had to explain, the better.

"Call me Kade."

When his strong, warm fingers wrapped around hers, a tingle shot up her arm. With a gasp, she jerked away. So much for acting unaffected. "Sorry," she said, trying to cover her confusion. "Static electric shock."

"Or something." The grin on Kade's face nearly sent her into a tailspin. He was flirting with her. She was not falling into his trap again.

"Anyway, nice to meet you. I have—things to do." She knew she was babbling, and the warmth of a blush moved up her cheeks.

"You okay, Pansy?" Micah's concerned voice prodded her into action.

"I'm just dandy." She'd continue to babble if she stood here looking at a man that was once the most important person in her life. "Gotta go." She turned and fled through the kitchen and out the back door. What she wanted to do was climb into her car and drive back to the anonymity of Denver.

No way that was going to happen.

She'd promised to take care of the café and pastry shop for Cary until the baby arrived, and she wouldn't go back on her word. Cary had asked Pansy about staying on permanently. That wonderful idea had just flown the coop.

She wasn't strong enough to spend two months around Kade. She wasn't sure she could spend two days around the cowboy without falling for him again.

Pansy was committed to staying in East Hope for another six weeks at the minimum, and she wouldn't go back on her word.

It was going to be a long six weeks.

Pulling in a deep breath, she let it out slowly. Unlike Kade, she'd never been a quitter. She's survived things worse than this. Much worse.

She'd always known she'd run into him someday, but she'd hoped that day was a long way off. Should have known better. For the past seven years nothing in her life had been easy.

One thing she could count on—Kade never stayed long in one place. Moving on was as natural to him as breathing. No way was he going to become a homebody now.

This might be a small town, and it might take some doing, but she'd stay out of his way. One short nod sealed her decision. It was going to take more than charm on Kade's part to move back into her life.

Keeping her distance from the cowboy had just become her first priority. "Kade Vaughn, you're not going to ride in here and mess up my life again."

Leaning against the old building, the worn bricks warm against her back, she surveyed the area. Turning her attention to the view across from the café, she lifted her shoulders then relaxed the muscles.

Groups of wild sunflowers bloomed among the sagebrush. The snow capped peaks of Three Sisters provided a beautiful backdrop to the high desert landscape.

Pansy fisted her hands and planted them on her hips. "This is my town now." No more running—not from her memories, and especially, not from Kade Vaughn.

~*~

Kade pulled his shiny new Dodge pickup beneath the

Cottonwood tree in front of Micah and Cary's farmhouse and turned off the key. When he'd walked into the Five and Diner to wait for Micah and had seen Pansy instead, he'd been speechless. She was every bit as beautiful as he remembered.

The wig had confused him for a moment, but nothing she could have done would throw him off for long. When Micah had introduced them, he'd recognized the panic in her expression. Dread had filled her pale blue eyes. Eyes that had haunted his dreams for years.

Kade jumped at a knock on his truck window. There stood his cousin with a goofy grin on his face. It was good to see Micah smile. The years of being married to his first wife, Marlene, had just about scrubbed any happiness from Micah's life. Thanks to Cary, Micah's grin was back.

"Where's your head? I've been standing here waiting for you come conscious." Micah stepped back as Kade opened the door and slid out of the truck.

"I'm mentally counting all the money I haven't won since Swamp Fox decided to dance on my hat." Kade rested his hand on the truck fender and paused a second for the rush of dizziness to pass. "I figure I'm down at least ten thousand dollars."

Micah reached out and touched Kade's arm. "You all right?"

"Yeah. My awesomeness just overpowers me sometimes." The dizzy spells were getting farther apart and less intense, but they snuck up on him once in a while, especially when he overdid. Kade started up the steps with Micah right behind.

"Cary's got lunch ready, but before we go in, I've got to ask you something."

Kade looked at his buddy. Not a hint of a grin marred Micah's face now.

"What's going on with you and Pansy?"

"What do you mean? She serves a great breakfast." It had been obvious Pansy hadn't wanted Micah to know there was something between them. He'd thought he'd covered his feelings pretty well at the café.

"I saw the look on her face when I introduced you two." Micah sat on the step and leaned back on his elbows. "Sit."

Kade hadn't had time to figure out his feelings for Pansy. All he knew at this point was the feelings were there, and they were as strong as ever. How long had it been since he'd seen her? They'd graduated from the University of Montana seven years ago. Seven years since he'd left home and lost track of her.

Hardest decision he'd ever made had been to leave Pansy, and he'd wondered often enough if he'd made the right one. They'd been so good together. Should have turned out different, but he'd never been able to figure out how.

"Let's just say we have history." He'd been little more than a kid, hadn't experienced life yet. He'd needed to see if he had what it took to ride bulls with the best. "With emphasis on the history part."

"The look on that woman's face wasn't indifference."

"Hey, I don't meddle in your life. I don't ask about you and Cary." That should do it. Micah had always been a private person, and he'd respect Kade's need to keep his feelings to himself.

"Cary's worried. You can tell me, or you can tell her." For the first time since they'd started this conversation, Micah smiled. "I'd choose me."

Micah was right about one thing. His wife was very protective of her friends, and if Kade wanted to stay here until he was healthy enough to go back on the road, he'd have to answer Cary's questions. "We'd just graduated from the U of M, and Pansy wanted to get married, you know, settle down and have kids. My plan was to go on the road and ride bulls for a living. When I told her marriage was out of the question right then, she fell apart."

"She wouldn't wait?"

"We didn't get to that. She wanted to set a date, and I couldn't give her one." The sight of her tear-stained face just before he'd walked away had haunted his dreams. He hadn't wanted to deal with her broken heart or his load of guilt, so he'd immersed himself in life on the road.

In the back of his mind, he'd always planned to come home to Pansy. He'd tried to tell her that before he left. At least he'd thought he had. "I texted her every few days and called at least once a week." Things had been, if not perfect, at least getting better.

Micah remained silent.

"The last time I talked to her she was so angry. She called me a selfish bastard and hung up on me." Kade had been confused. Pansy had always been the calm one, tending to think things through and find a solution."

"And you haven't seen her since until today?"

"Took me two years before I came home. When I finally did, she was gone." Knowing her parents the way he did, Kade wasn't surprised she'd left and hadn't told them where she was going. But none of their friends had heard from her either. That did surprise him.

The girl he'd known then had been big into community and friendship, loyal to the bone. Sure, she'd been angry and hurt when he hadn't wanted to get married, but to give up everything and disappear. It wasn't like his Pansy.

Guess he didn't have the right to call her his any more.

"Through the years, off and on, I tried to find her. I can't believe all I have to do is get hurt and come here to the outback of Oregon and there she is." Micah's invitation to convalesce at the ranch had been just what he'd needed. He'd have gone stir-crazy living at home with his parents. No concussion was a good one, and his had been pretty bad.

He'd mostly recovered. Now he looked normal, and he'd regained most of his balance. The doctors said no more bull riding—ever, but those doctors didn't know Kade Vaughn.

He'd been having a magical year, one that every competitor in any sport dreamed of. For the first four months of the TBC season, he'd been damn near perfect. He'd won over half of the events he'd entered and he'd been second at several more. Yup, he'd been flying high right up until Swamp Fox threw him into the fence and knocked him out.

A week in the hospital then a month living with his parents had him crawling out of his skin. Even though he was one of the lucky ones, and his parents loved him and wanted the best for him, they'd hovered. His mom had been a wreck every time he left the house.

Micah's invitation had come just soon enough to save his sanity.

"I appreciate you and Cary letting me stay, don't think I don't, but Pansy and I have to work this out by ourselves, if we can."

Micah stood and stretched before turning to Kade. "You're always welcome here, you know that. Just know, if you hurt Pansy in any way my wife will kill you." He turned and moved to the top step then looked over his shoulder at Kade. "Let's go in. Cary has lunch ready. Think you can eat after that breakfast?"

"I can always eat. You know that." Kade followed Micah through the house to the kitchen. "You don't think she'd poison me, do you?"

"Cary? She's not a sneak. She'll give you fair warning before she comes after you."

"Good to know," Kade said as they entered the huge ranch kitchen.

Micah's wife stood in front of the stove, her very pregnant belly resting against the appliance. She turned and smiled. "Tomato soup and cheese sandwiches." She tipped the pan and slid a sandwich onto a plate with four others. "Sit."

"Yes, ma'am." Kade dropped into one of the oak chairs that ringed the table and turned to Micah. "She have everyone around here trained to sit on command?"

Before Micah could answer, Cary turned and pointed the spatula in their direction. "You'd better think carefully about your answer."

Micah looked from Cary to Kade. "There's not a right way to answer your question, so I'll start on this delicious soup." He picked up his spoon and took a spoonful. "Mmmmm."

"Smart man." Kade took a sandwich off the plate Cary had set on the table. The warm cheese and toasty bread melted in his mouth. "Thanks, Cary. How's the little guy?"

In a move he'd seen many pregnant women make, Cary laid her hand on the front of her stomach. As she looked down, a sweet smile graced her face. She raised her gaze to Kade's. "We don't know if it's a boy or girl. We're going to be surprised."

"Okay, how's the little person doing?"

Cary placed her hands on the small of her back and stretched. "The little person better get here soon. This baby's about to break my ribs when it stretches."

Kade had seen his sister pregnant and a couple of cousins, but he'd been gone most of the time. He'd show up long enough to play Uncle Kade then hit the road again. Birth was something he'd just as soon not think about.

Cary raised her gaze to meet his, the loving expression gone. "Micah says you met my best friend at the café."

"I did. She's different. You've got to admit you don't see Cleopatra in East Hope every day."

"She's had a tough time." Cary glared at him. "Micah's told me about you. You stay away from her."

"Cary, this isn't any of our business." Micah rose and pulled his wife into a hug. "Kade's promised to be good."

He hadn't exactly promised anything, but the last thing Kade wanted to do was make Cary mad. She'd been kind enough to invite him into their home at a time when she probably didn't need any guests.

Cary brought a two-layer cake to the table, the pink frosting piled into fluffy mounds around the top. "Sorry, I tend to fly off the handle before I think these days." She pulled two plates from the cupboard and put a large serving of cake on each.

Kade took a bite and got lost in the sensation of sweet. Cary was a genius when it came to cakes and pastries. Her voice brought him back.

"Pansy was a friend when I needed one. She's still helping." Cary pinched a bit of cake between her fingers and popped it into her mouth. "She's offered to run the café until the baby gets here."

"If you don't mind my asking, how did you two meet?" Kade inhaled the cherry cake and wondered if he dared ask for more.

Micah reached across the table, cut two more large pieces of cake and flopped one on Kade's plate. "Nobody can eat just one serving of Cary's sweets."

Cary sank into a chair, lowering her bulk carefully. She ran her hands through her spiky, white-blonde hair then leaned back. "I was living in Denver, trying to earn enough money to pay my tuition at Cordon Bleu. Pansy came to work at Chez Romeo about a week after I did, and we hit it off right away."

Kade took another bite and chewed slowly. Be cool. "How long ago was that?"

Micah watched him, his eyebrows raised.

"We'd worked there about two years before I came here. Three years ago, I guess." Cary tipped her head and squinted. "You seem very interested in Pansy."

Kade stood and carried his dishes to the sink. "Do you want me to wash these?" He turned to find both Wests looking at him. "What, hasn't a guest offered to help before?"

Cary and Micah burst out laughing.

"Nice deflection," Micah said. "But not good enough. If you think you can ask about my wife's best friend and not have her question you about your motives, think again." He put his arm around Cary's shoulder and gave her a quick kiss on the lips.

The look she gave Micah filled Kade with a hot spurt of regret followed by the cold feeling of loss. There had been a time Pansy had looked at him like that, a time he'd been everything to her.

Could he get that back? Did he want to? The idea was intriguing, and something he'd have to think about when he was alone.

If he wasn't careful, she might run. He'd been given the chance to connect with Pansy again. He didn't want to blow it.

"You've got to admit she's a fascinating woman." Kade looked into Cary's eyes, trying to portray sincerity.

"Yes, and?" Cary's hands went to her hips, or at least where her hips used to be.

"It can't hurt to get to know her a little better, right?" He already knew Pansy better than anyone. At least, he had known her then.

Cary circled the table and put her hand on Kade's shoulder. "You're leaving soon. Don't start something you can't finish. Pansy's never said, but something or someone hurt her badly. And I don't want to see that happen again."

Kade took her hand in his. "I won't. I promise."

She nodded then turned to her husband. "Micah, I feel a nap coming on." She gave him a peck on the cheek and left the room.

"Think about what Cary said." Micah stacked the plates in the sink.

"I'd never hurt her." The word *again* was left unspoken, but Kade felt it reverberate against his skull.

The vision of Pansy standing beside the horse trailer at their last college rodeo filled his mind. She'd been so excited when she'd won the barrel race. When he'd told her he was leaving her behind, that he was going on the road to ride bulls for a living, he'd broken her heart. That was something he'd regret 'til his dying day.

Micah's look said his lies weren't working. "Maybe you should just leave her alone. There's plenty of other women around here who would love to date a champion bull rider."

"So now you get to tell me who I can talk to?" He should have agreed with his cousin. He should have been able to walk away without a care, but caring about Pansy was something he'd never given up.

Micah's slow smile made him mad.

This man spent years with a woman the devil wouldn't have given a second glance to, and he was going to tell Kade how to live his life? No way.

Kade drew his finger through a glob of frosting on his plate before stacking it in the sink. He turned to face Micah. "Fine. I'll leave the dress-up doll alone. Will that make you happy?"

CHAPTER TWO

As she plated the latest lunch order, Pansy caught sight of herself in the big mirror on the kitchen wall. Her carrot red wig was pulled into curls on top of her head. She smoothed the full skirt of her navy blue polka dot housedress and touched the snowy white collar.

Retro fit her new personality like a tailored jacket. With bright red lipstick and long black false eyelashes, she'd come as close as she could to recreating Lucy Ricardo. The redhead's feisty spirit was something she channeled when knew she'd have a trying day.

She used her hip to open the swinging door into the dining room then placed heaping plates in front of Henry and Cheney, two of her regular customers.

"Can't complain of too little food when you do the cooking, Miss Pansy," Cheney said.

"Need more coffee?" Pansy had filled Cheney's cup to the brim when the bell over the door rang for the fourth time in the last few minutes. Tempted to rip the damned thing off the wall, she stopped and drew in a breath.

For the past six days, she'd jumped every time the café door opened thinking she'd see Kade's smiling face. The tension was making her batty as a bucket calf at feeding time.

At the sight of the tiny woman waving her fingers, Pansy couldn't help but smile. "Hi, Mrs. LeBeouf."

"Now honey. You just call me Wanda Lu. Friends don't call friends by their last names." The caustic scent of old school Aqua Net hairspray overlaid with the spicy aroma of Tabu perfume surrounded the little woman like a dense fog. Wisps of coal-black hair had been teased to add several inches to the miniscule woman's height. A couple of strands had escaped the lacquer to float around her head.

Wanda Lu stopped, plopped her hands on her hips and tsked at Pansy. "It's nothing to be ashamed of, you know, not knowing how to do your own hair, but that doesn't mean you have to wear a wig all the time. I'm as big a Lucille Ball fan as anyone, but y'all come on in to Wanda Lu's Locks, and I'll show you a simple do. One even a youngster like you can master."

What was Pansy supposed to say to that? "Thank you for the offer, but..." *But I don't want to look like Dolly Parton's poor relation.* "Let's find you a place to sit. The special today is chicken-fried steak and home fries." Since being in East Hope, Pansy had learned a universal truth about small town cafes—you couldn't have too much fried food.

Wanda Lu followed Pansy to the booth in the corner.

As soon as she sat down, the hairdresser pulled off one of her vintage high-top Reeboks and rubbed the ball of her foot with gnarled fingers. "Danged bunions. Got 'em from standing on my feet all day, you know. Watch out or they'll get you, too." She slipped her shoe back on and slid to the middle of the seat. Her feet swung a few inches from the black and white linoleum floor, gently bumping the plywood base of the bench.

"I'll have your coffee in just a minute." Pansy opened a menu and placed it in front of Wanda Lu. "You just give me a wave when you're ready to order."

Pansy left the elderly woman perusing the menu and made her way back to the counter. As she lifted the coffee pot to refill Henry's cup, the bell rang again.

Mother of all things holy! The doorway to the café was filled with Wranglers and muscles and cool gray eyes. Kade had aged well, if she could call twenty-nine aging. The lines of his face had thinned, his muscles were more defined. She found it hard to look away.

What was wrong with her brain? She was hardworking, smart and knew enough to take care of herself. Why did the mere sight of this man turn her into a five-year-old coveting a candy bar?

Without acknowledging the cowboy, Pansy turned to the two older gentlemen at the counter. "Refill?"

Henry Potter nodded his shiny, bald head then pushed his cup toward her without saying a word.

"I'd love one, Miss Pansy." Cheney Mills gave her a nearly toothless grin. "Did I ever tell you about the time the cougar came right in the front door of our old farmhouse when I was a kid?"

"She doesn't want to hear that old lie." Henry pulled his cup closer and turned to his friend. "Besides, she's been in town long enough to have heard all your stories several times."

Cheney leaned back, almost falling off the barstool, and jabbed Henry in the shoulder with a bony finger. "You don't know that. Pansy loves hearing my stories."

"Stop poking me, you old reprobate." Henry swiveled until he faced Cheney.

"And if I don't?"

"Now gentlemen." One thing Pansy didn't need today was an octogenarian fistfight.

Kade crossed the room and stood between the two men. He laid one hand on each of their shoulders. "Every time I see you two, you're arguing about something." He raised his gaze to meet Pansy's. "But I guess Miss Pansy is as good a thing to argue about as any."

Pansy's chest tightened as she tried to pull in a breath. She was struggling for something to say when Wanda Lu appeared at Kade's elbow.

"Come on, you cute thing, you." Wanda Lu's face dissolved into creases when she smiled, her orange lipstick bleeding into the wrinkles around her lips. She grabbed hold of Kade's arm and pulled him toward two empty stools. "Have you met our Pansy?"

Pansy gave him a short nod. "Mr. Vaughn."

"It's Kade." Kade shot a grin at Pansy then turned his attention back to Wanda Lu. "Micah introduced us the other day."

"I been trying to talk this guy into being my boy toy for years." Wanda Lu's arthritic fingers wrapped around Kade's arm as she beamed up at him. "But he just wants to be friends."

Kade looked down at the older woman. "I keep trying to tell you, you're too much woman for me."

Wanda Lu turned to Pansy, a wide grin on her face. "I'm what they call a cougar. I always thought my spirit animal was a big cat."

Pansy scrubbed at a non-existent spot on the counter, trying to control her laughter.

Wanda Lu held up her hand to the side of her mouth as she turned back to Kade. "I heard she wears those wigs because of the cancer. The chemo ate up all her hair. Heard she's bald as old Henry over there beneath them but lucky to be alive. Don't know if that's true, so don't quote me."

Did the older woman think she couldn't hear?

Wanda Lu and Kade stood less than three feet from her.

Pansy opened her mouth then closed it again. Rumors had been flying since the day she'd arrived as to why she wore wigs and where she got her outlandish costumes. Pansy wasn't about to get into her personal business to set them straight.

Kade's head jerked up, and he stared into Pansy's eyes, a fleeting expression that could be fear crossing his face. When she didn't respond, he shrugged and put his hand on Wanda Lu's. "It'd probably be better if we didn't spread gossip. Tell me what you were up to while I was on the road."

"You're right about the rumors." Wanda Lu grasped the edge of the counter and spun herself back and forth on the stool, her tangerine nail polish bright against the white Formica. "Nothing special going on with me, but I heard you had some excitement. Heard that nasty old bull almost killed you."

Almost killed? Pansy's heart sprinted in her chest, trying to outrun the panic coursing through her veins. A world without Kade was unthinkable!

No, she wasn't going there.

Wanda Lu squinted in her direction. "Lost my glasses again, but I don't need to see the menu here. I'll have the special." She turned to Kade. "What do you want, hot stuff? I'm buying."

"No you're not. You bought last time." With a wink at Pansy, he fixed his attention on the small woman. "It's my turn."

Pansy couldn't help herself. She was still shaken by the thought of Kade dying. "You almost got killed?"

A strange expression flickered across the cowboy's face. Regret, or anger, maybe? She couldn't be sure.

"Nah. Just banged me up a little. Comes with the job."

"Then you need to find another job." She reached for her order pad in the pocket of her dress, keeping her eyes fixed on the small tablet. "What can I get you, Mr. Vaughn?"

Kade kept his eyes on her face. "What's good? And it's Kade."

What's good? Certainly not the feelings bubbling up from a cauldron of old memories. It was time to put some distance between her and Mr. Vaughn. She'd hoped when she saw Kade again, his presence wouldn't throw her into a spin, but just call her the Tasmanian devil. "Everything."

"I'll take the special, too."

With a nod, Pansy escaped to the kitchen. She really needed to get a grip. This must be what addiction felt like. You knew it wasn't good for you, but you couldn't help yourself. Time to remember what had happened the last time she'd given her heart to Kade Vaughn.

When she'd needed him the most, he'd been nowhere to be found.

She'd serve his meal like he was any other customer. He was Mr. Vaughn now, not the boy she'd loved and lost.

After pan-frying the steaks, she smothered them with gravy, heaped on the fries and carried the loaded plates out to Wanda Lu and Kade.

Only Kade's seat was empty.

Pansy settled one plate in front of Wanda Lu then looked around the room. The cowboy wasn't in sight. "Where did your friend go?"

Wands Lu pulled her plate closer and doused the food with pepper. After taking a bite, she chewed then swallowed. "He had something he had to do. This is real good." Wanda Lu added more pepper then took another bite.

"Is he coming back?"

"He said to box his up. He'll be back later."

Pansy took the plate into the kitchen and scraped the contents into a heap in a Styrofoam box. She set it in the industrial size refrigerator then sank into the old oak chair beside the door.

Kade was gone—again.

Leaving her to pick up the pieces. His pattern hadn't altered in all this time. Sure, this time it wasn't so important.

This time it was only a dinner, not a baby.

~*~

Cancer? Could Wanda Lu be right? Why hadn't he tried harder to find Pansy?

Because, for a big, tough man who rode bulls for a living, he was a big ol'coward. He didn't have the guts to watch pain fill her eyes when he told her he still didn't want to settle down, still wasn't husband material. He'd handed Wanda Lu a ten to cover his meal and fled.

Leaning against the faded brick wall at the side of the East Hope Savings and Loan, he looked down the quiet main street of his adopted hometown. It hadn't changed much since the first time he'd been here when he was twelve. The same stores were in the same buildings. The same people ran them.

"Kade. Are you standing on the street waiting for a pretty woman to take you to lunch?" Millie's bright blue eyes contrasted with her candy apple red hair. She and her husband had owned the local grocery store for as long as he could remember.

"Nah, just waiting for the action to start." Kade stood and put his arm around Millie's shoulder. "Good to see you again, sweetheart."

"You're in for a long wait if you're waiting for action in this town." Millie gave him a quick hug then took his hand and pulled him toward the café. "I'm in bad need of a cup of coffee and a piece Cary's pie."

He'd just run out on lunch. Now wasn't the time to go back in and face Pansy. "Oh, hey, no. Can't." Kade pulled his fingers free and stepped back. "Got things to do."

Millie snorted. "Like you're busy. You're here to recuperate from that bang to your noggin. Clinton talked to Cary and got your whole story." She pulled the door open and stood back waiting for Kade to enter.

He'd learned long ago not to cross Millie. She'd been part mother and part warden when he'd spent time in East Hope with Micah as a youth. She'd back you up unless you screwed up. Then she was a kid's worst nightmare. He hadn't been in Millie's sights for years, but he was sure she could be an adult's nightmare, too.

He could be thickheaded, but he wasn't stupid. "I'd love to have a cup with the prettiest woman in town." He followed Millie to an empty booth.

A faded black and white photo of John Wayne shaking an elderly man's hand hung on the wall above the booth, right beside a poster advertising the 1938 Pendleton rodeo. He'd just stuffed his keys into his pocket and slid onto the bench when a plastic menu slapped onto the table in front of him with a *thwack*.

Pansy stood beside the booth, looking like an angry angel, her blue eyes snapping with irritation.

She turned to Millie, sat a full mug of coffee in front of the older woman and ignored Kade completely. "What can I get you, Millie?"

"I was thinking of cherry raspberry pie, but I gotta watch my figure." Millie grinned as she looked from Kade to Pansy and back. "The coffee's enough. I just need a little pick-me-up."

With a nod, Pansy turned and returned to the kitchen.

Millie shook her head. "Poor girl. I heard she tried a do-it-yourself hair color, and it burned up all her hair follicles. That's why she wears the wigs."

First it was cancer—he'd been worried about that, but now a bad dye job? The locals must be having a ball trying to figure out why anyone as pretty as Pansy would wear those outrageous wigs and costumes. Kade almost laughed out loud until he saw the dead serious look on Millie's face. "Who'd you hear this from? Wanda Lu?"

"Wanda Lu wouldn't know the truth if it bit her on that big old tush of hers." Millie reached up and smoothed an errant curl into place then took a sip of her coffee. She sat the cup on the table with a clunk and pointed a red-tipped finger at Kade. "That woman's the biggest gossip in town."

"So Pansy told you?"

Millie straightened her shoulders. Indignation washed over her face. "I'd never ask so personal a question. The poor girl's probably embarrassed as heck to have made a mistake like that."

"Then who?"

Millie didn't elaborate, and when Kade glanced up, she'd developed an all-encompassing interest in wiping a smudge from her glasses.

Something white flashed by his face and landed with a plop in front of him. The top of a Styrofoam container popped open exposing cold chicken-fried steak and fries topped with congealing gravy. A blob of the thick brown goo landed on the leg of his jeans.

"You forgot this the last time you were here." Pansy slapped a receipt on the table beside the food.

Even the full, gathered skirt of the '50s housedress she wore couldn't hide the enticing way her hips swayed with each step as she hurried back to the kitchen.

He'd missed watching Pansy move, and he appreciated the sight of her long legs below the hem of the dress, but put that girl in Wranglers and cowboy boots and she was a showstopper.

Millie cleared her throat, and Kade drew his attention back to his lunch partner. "I see the famous Kade Vaughn charm is at work again." Her too familiar smirk was firmly in place.

"So, you and Clinton Barnes, huh?" Time to get the spotlight off him and back on someone else. It was good to see Pansy again, but he wasn't going to be here that long, and he sure didn't need to get involved with an old girlfriend. Make that *the* old girlfriend.

Kade cut the corner off the steak and took a bite. Even cold, it was good.

Millie's cheeks flushed pink. She took a big swallow of coffee. After patting her lips with the napkin, she fumbled through her purse and reapplied her pale pink lipstick.

"You're stalling." Now was not the time to let Millie

off the hook. The woman had been alone long enough. Her husband had been dead for almost ten years. He was glad to see she'd found happiness with a great guy.

Her eyes softened and a smile lit her lips. "Clinton is . . ." Millie twisted a tissue into a pile of fluffy bits. She raised her gaze to meet Kade's. "He's the best thing that's happened to me in a long time. Now that's enough about me. Have you got a girl?"

"You know better than that. I don't have time for a girlfriend. I travel too much." He dipped a fry into the gravy. He was hungrier than he'd thought. "Gotta win that world championship before I get too old."

"Pffft." She waved a hand, dismissing his opinion. "You're a kid. You got your whole life ahead of you."

"Not riding bulls, I don't. I've only got a couple years left." Kade's shoulders slumped with his sigh. Since the day when he was ten and had watched Adriano Moraes ride, he'd been working toward becoming a TBC world champion.

Being a year-end winner in the Top Bulls and Cowboys Association was his life long goal. He'd been close last year until Swamp Fox had thrown him off in the tenth round of the finals, stomping his dream into the dirt.

Kade dropped the fry back into the container, his appetite gone. If he didn't rise to the occasion in the next few years, he'd be too old. And then what would he do?

A bull rider was all he'd ever wanted to be. When he couldn't ride any more, and that day was coming faster than he liked, who would he be? Just a plain old broken down cowboy, that's who.

"Hey, girlie," Millie shouted, her high voice shrill above the noise of the other patrons. "Pansy Lark!" She continued to hold her hand above her head, waving her fingers at the waitress as she looked back at Kade. "I just love that name, don't you?"

Great, he was wallowing in self-pity, while Millie called Pansy over to watch. He sucked in a breath and straightened. The woman he'd known before would have consoled him, but this Pansy wasn't his Pansy any more. She'd probably laugh her ass of at his misery.

The smile Pansy gave Millie was filled with warmth. "What do you need? More coffee?" She reached for Millie's cup.

Millie put her hand over the cup, shaking her head. "I forgot to tell you about Cary's shower. I talked to Wanda Lu. Will next Wednesday at 6pm work for you?"

"Sure. Where did you decide to have it?" Pansy stood with her body angled away from Kade not bothering to look at him. "What can I bring?"

"Micah said we could use the ranch. The weather is supposed to be nice, so we'll have it outside." Millie scooted to the edge of the seat and stood. "Can you bring those ribs you barbequed for the Fourth of July celebration?"

"Sure. How many have you invited?"

"Just the important folks, ten women and eight men."

"Men?" Pansy shot Kade a look. "I thought this was a baby shower for Cary."

Millie laughed. "Well, it's Micah's baby too, and you know this town never passes up a party." Millie stood and gave Pansy a quick hug. "See you two later. Don't do anything I wouldn't do." With a grin, she hurried out of the café.

Time for him to make his escape. Kade stood and pulled a twenty out of his wallet and dropped in onto the table. "Keep the change."

Pansy stared off into space, not acknowledging him, her body tense.

He laid his hand on her arm. "You okay?"

At his touch, she jerked away, swiping her fingers across her cheek to wipe away a tear.

CHAPTER THREE

Driving less than twenty-five miles an hour put off arriving at the baby shower for a few minutes, but there was no escaping the inevitable. A bright pink and blue bag rested on the seat beside Pansy, the baby gift inside.

Three pans of her special barbequed ribs seemed like a lot, but no matter how many she made, the only thing left in the pans at the end of any function were streaks of sauce.

She'd tried on several outfits before deciding on her Marilyn Monroe wig and low-cut dress. Marilyn was one of the most determined women she'd researched, and Pansy wore the costume like a shield.

When Millie and Wanda Lu suggested giving Cary a baby shower, Pansy'd reluctantly agreed. Cary was her best friend, and this was Cary's first pregnancy. She could buck up and get through this get-together, pretending to be happy.

Finding out Kade would be attending the party had thrown her into a tailspin. Their baby, their little girl, would have been six years old next month. The miscarriage two months before her due date didn't make the pain of losing Maxie any less real.

After putting in an appearance and saying hi to everyone, she'd plead a headache. Less than an hour of pretending to be normal and she'd be home alone—again. Just the way she liked it.

The small pasture beside the ranch house was already filled with cars, trucks and Byron's Harley. Folding chairs were scattered around the lawn, and beside the porch sat a big aluminum trough filled with ice and cans of pop and beer.

A long table loaded with salads and vegetables was in the center of the lawn, and a smaller round table was stacked with pink and blue cupcakes.

Pansy grabbed one pan of ribs in each hand and turned toward the house.

Kade blocked her way. With a grin, he took hold of the pans.

"I can get these." She straightened her shoulders and reminded herself to remain calm. She tugged on the pans with care. The last thing she needed was for him to drop them.

He lifted them out of her reach.

Jumping to try to take the pans from him wasn't an option she was willing to stoop to, so she shot him a look that should have scorched the brim of his Stetson.

His grin widened.

An hour was going to be too long if she couldn't get away from him.

"I'll just hold them while you get the last one then I'll stack all three in your arms, and you can carry them to the house by yourself." He tried to erase the humor from his expression, faking sincerity. "Nobody can say I stand in the way of a strong woman."

Strong woman. She'd been young and so naïve when she'd been in college. She was strong now, because she hadn't had a choice. It was toughen up or die in her world.

He didn't seem to get the message that she didn't want him around. He'd run before when she'd been needy, maybe he'd stay true to form.

She channeled Marilyn, turning on the charm. "Why thank you. I'd love your help." She relinquished the pans and pulled the last one from the back of the car. Turning, she wedged the third pan beneath Kade's arm, hoping it wouldn't tip and run barbeque sauce down the side of his shirt. She didn't hope very hard, though.

Placing her hand on his other elbow, she moved him toward the farmhouse. The look on his face was priceless, and if she hadn't been set on playing a role, she'd have laughed.

As they approached the porch, Cary waved from one of the white wooden Adirondack chairs, her other hand resting on her extended belly. "You'll have to come up here. I'm not standing again until it's time to open the presents."

"Let me get these ribs on the table, and I'll be back." Pansy took the pan from beneath Kade's arm. "Follow me, and you can put those big muscles to some good use."

"Me and my big muscles are right behind you, boss." Kade followed her into the kitchen where Cary had left several platters on the counter.

Pansy emptied the first pan of ribs onto one. She pushed another toward Kade. "Put those on this plate. We'll leave the last one covered to keep it warm." She licked sauce off her fingers then looked up to see him watching her.

"What?"

He shook his head and busied himself with the task of plating the ribs. "You're just mighty pretty in that outfit."

"Jeez, you sound like a character from an old time western."

"How about if I say you're a knock-out? Or you're hot?"

She handed him one of the platters and picked up the other. "How about if we go to the party and stop talking about me?" Damn that man! She couldn't quite contain the smile that broke out on her face. She'd almost made it to the porch when she heard his voice.

"You look great as a blonde."

She whirled, almost dropping the ribs. "What does that mean?"

Kade caught up to her at the door. "I like you as Lucy better than Cleopatra. Not that I don't appreciate Cleo." He pushed the screen door open with his hip and held it for her to pass through. "But Marilyn is my all time favorite."

As she walked away, she called back to him. "You haven't seen Cat Woman yet."

~*~

"Ho-ly shit!" The words slipped out as visions of Pansy, her curves encased in a skin-tight, black vinyl catsuit pummeled his brain.

"Holy shit, what?" Micah's voice broke into his imaginings with a jolt.

Oh, yeah. He was a class act, lusting after Pansy at a baby shower. He managed to pull himself back to the present and turned to his friend. "Nothing, nothing at all."

Micah looked to where Pansy was dishing out ribs then back to Kade. "Sure, buddy. I believe you."

Kade made his way as casually as he could to the food table. Not an easy task with visions of Pansy in black running through his mind. Moving the condiments to the side, he made room for the platter of ribs.

He looked for Pansy, and found her talking to Byron Garrett, one of Micah's long time cowhands. The big man had come to Oregon from Texas several years ago and claimed he'd found a home. When Byron laughed at something Pansy said jealousy raw and rank rushed through his body.

Pansy laid her hand on Byron's arm and smiled up at him.

Nobody was going to flirt with Kade Vaughn's Cat Woman while he stood back and watched. He'd only taken one step toward the two before he felt a hand on his arm.

Cheney Mills stood beside him, his tobacco-stained smile firmly in place. "Saw you gazin' at that pretty Pansy. She's a looker all right." The rumpled old man patted Kade's arm with his boney fingers, nodding his head as he spoke. "Mighty fine one for sure."

The rumor mill of East Hope was alive and well, and if he weren't careful, he'd be their main grist. "She seems nice. I don't know her very well." Kade took a step away from the little man, but Cheney followed like he was attached with a chain.

"Too bad about her hair, though." Cheney ran his fingers through his shock of white hair then gave his head another sympathy-filled shake.

Kade didn't want to get involved with any more speculation on Pansy's wigs, but call him shallow, he was curious as to what the town would come up with this time. "I heard she was sick, and I heard she used bad hair dye. Which is it?"

Cheney wrinkled his nose and waved a hand at his young friend's ignorance. "Who's passing those unfounded rumors? That's not what happened at all."

"And you know the truth?" he asked. He should stop this conversation right now. He had every intention until he looked up to see Pansy laughing with cowboy.

Byron pulled her into a hug.

Well, to hell with saving Pansy's hair styling reputation. When he returned his attention to Cheney, the wizened old man was practically levitating with excitement. Kade rested one hand on Cheney's shoulder to keep him grounded. Wouldn't want the old man to lift off before he got this load of hot air off his chest.

Cheney held his hand up to the side of his mouth. "Miss Pansy used to be fat, poor girl. A year ago, just before she came to East Hope, she went on a diet where all she ate was grapefruit and diet soda. She dropped the pounds, all right, but she lost her hair in the process. Improper diet will do that, you know."

He stared at the old man, his skinny chest wheezing with delight at having the very latest in gossip. Like this man knew anything about nutrition.

The grin dropped off Cheney's face, and Kade realized he'd tightened his grip. If he squeezed the old guy's shoulder any tighter, he'd break off a piece of the fragile bone. Relaxing, he dropped his arms to his sides.

Cheney ducked his head. "It's the truth. Got it from a reliable source."

"Maybe we should keep this story to ourselves."

"Hey, I ain't no Flibbertigibbet." Cheney snorted in disgust and turned to walk away. He took several steps before turning back to Kade. "I just thought you liking her and all, you should know. I won't make that mistake again."

What the hell? Every small town had its share of characters, but East Hope seemed to be the gathering place for misfits. He turned his attention back to Pansy, only to see her still standing too close to Byron for his liking. Time to put a stop to this.

In three long strides, he crossed the yard. "Hey, buddy." He grabbed Byron's hand and shook, squeezing more than necessary.

Confusion flitted across the big ranch hand's face followed by irritation. Byron squeezed back and with hands the size of dinner plates he nearly crushed Kade's fingers.

Good thing I don't have to get on a bull for a while.

With as much finesse as he could manage, he pulled his hand from Byron's and slapped the big man on the shoulder. "How's things going?"

"Fine." Byron's brows drew together. He shrugged, stepped out of Kade's reach then turned to Pansy. "Y'all have a nice day now."

As the cowboy walked away, Pansy snickered. "You showed him."

Kade realized he was flexing the fingers of his right hand and dropped his arm to his side. "Thank god he didn't want to arm wrestle. I'm a better lover than a fighter, especially with someone the size of an Angus bull."

Before Pansy could make him feel lower, a clanging noise got everyone's attention. Millie stood on the porch holding the triangle used to call the ranch hands to eat. She gave it one more bang before moving to the top of the steps.

"I see some of you aren't done eating, so go ahead and finish. We're going to have Cary and Micah start opening their baby's presents."

Micah's eight-year-old daughter scampered down the porch steps, jumping off the last two to land next to Kade. She looked up and her freckled face was filled with excitement. "Oh, boy, presents for my little brother or sister. You think maybe there's one for me?"

"There might just be one, Willa."

The little girl's pale red brows pulled together, and she put her tiny hands on her hips. "You haven't been here for a while, so I'll remind you. My name is Willa Wild. You wouldn't like it if I called you Ka."

Kade pursed his lips as if in thought then nodded. "You're right. A name is important. I'm sorry."

Cary grasped the handrail and waddled down the steps. Byron carried one of the Adirondack chairs to the lawn, and Cary sank into it. "This was supposed to be an opportunity for you all to meet our baby, but since the little bugger is two weeks late, we decided to go ahead. Willa Wild, will you bring me one of those?"

One by one, Cary and Micah opened the presents. The wrappings ranged from frothy pastel papers and curly bows to several brown paper bags. When Cary opened Pansy's gift, she grasped it to her chest, her eyes filling with tears. Pansy had looked for months before finding the vintage Moulin Roty children's baking set online.

"This is perfect," Cary said as she struggled to stand. "Boy or girl, my kid is going to learn how to bake."

"And me," Willa Wild chirped.

Cary reached out and pulled the redheaded little girl into her arms. "Willa Wild, you're already a master baker. We'll teach the baby together."

The redhead gave Cary a peck on the cheek then turned to the crowd. "I'm going to help bring the special present." She raced around the corner of the house, followed by Clinton and Millie.

Pansy gave her friend a long hug. "You're going to be a great mom." Her voice came out a whisper as she steeled her mind to keep the tears at bay.

Cary and Micah opened the remaining gifts while they waited for their daughter to come back. Many were handmade, ranging from baby blankets and layettes to a miniscule pair of buckaroo chaps and a tiny straw hat.

As Cary opened the last present, her daughter staggered back into the yard, carrying a saddle. It was for a small child, but was still an armful for the girl.

"This is from Clinton and Millie. It's too small for me," she chirped, dropping the saddle at her dad's feet. "But I'm going to teach our baby how to ride."

Micah took the saddle from his daughter and settled it onto the porch rail. "Our baby is one lucky kid to have you as a sister."

Willa hugged her dad then took off to find her friends.

As each gift was oohed and awed over, the lump in Pansy's throat had grown. When she saw the saddle, tears threatened to roll down her cheeks. She was happy for Cary and Micah, she really was. They were good people and they deserved the best. But this party drove home the fact that she'd never be able share her love of rodeo with her daughter. She'd never be able to share anything with her daughter.

I'm not going to cry. Not in front of all these people.

Crying demanded explanations, and she wasn't going to do that. Desperate to leave, she looked around for a way out without having to explain.

"You don't look so good."

At the top of her list of people who were never getting explanations was Kade. She kept her gaze on the grass. "I'm fine. Just a headache from all the sugar."

"They haven't served the cupcakes yet."

She turned around to face him. Her plan for keeping away from the cowboy wasn't going well. "What do you want?"

"Just trying to help."

"Well, don't."

"If I tell Cary and Micah you don't feel well, that I'm taking you home, you won't even have to talk to them. You won't have to talk to anyone."

Pansy blinked the tears back and cleared her throat. It was like he'd read her mind. "Ah, no." *Hell, no!*

She didn't want to go anywhere with Kade, but if she went to Cary herself and told her friend she had a headache, the Wests would insist she go upstairs and lay down for a while. They'd check on her every few minutes, and if she knew the townspeople of East Hope, they'd all end up in the bedroom with her.

If she insisted on going home, Cary would make sure Micah drove.

No matter how much she hated the thought of him helping her, going with Kade would get her away from the party without giving a reason for her departure. "Just a ride home."

"Get your stuff and get in the car. I'll explain to Micah." By the time she retrieved the roasting pans she'd used to bring the BBQ, Kade had talked to Micah and met her at the car. "Ready to go?"

Pansy placed the empty pans in the back seat. Pushing the door shut, she grabbed the handle on the driver's side of her green Ford Focus. The old car didn't look great, but she could count on it when she needed it.

That was more than she could say for many people in her life, including Kade.

"I told them you had a migraine. If you drive, they'll wonder what's up." He trained his gray eyes on her across the roof of the Focus. "You might want to rub the side of your head, cause they're all watching us."

He was right. Pansy put her fingers to her temples as she walked around the car and climbed in. When Kade had settled in the driver's seat, she asked, "Why are you doing this?"

"You didn't seem to be having much fun, so I thought I'd give you a way to leave gracefully." Kade handed her a paper bag he'd grabbed on the way to the car.

Pansy looked inside then pulled out a pretty pink cupcake with a tiny sugar baby bib on the top.

"I was having a great time."

"You always cry at baby showers?"

"I wasn't." She wanted to cry now. It would be so nice to tell Kade about Maxie. Tell him how she'd held her baby, talked to her and loved her beyond all reason. But the conversation would open up all kinds of problems and explanations, and she wasn't ready for that kind of drama. Not with this man. "Allergies."

"Right—about the cupcake? You going to keep them both for yourself?" He held his hand out, and she handed the pretty pink confection to him.

She pulled out the second cupcake, a blue one, and took a bite. Drowning her sorrows in sugar had never failed her before.

"When are you going to show me your catsuit?"

Pansy sucked in a breath and a bit of cake she'd just swallowed went down the wrong way. As she coughed uncontrollably, Kade pulled into a wide spot on the side of the road.

Finally gaining control, she pulled a tissue from the box in the console and wiped her eyes. When she could speak again without choking, she waved a hand at Kade. "Go."

"Sorry about that." Kade's grin said he wasn't sorry at all. "I didn't think you'd have that big of a reaction." He took a huge bite of his cupcake leaving a smudge of pink icing on his lip.

With very little effort, she could lean over and lick his lip clean.

Where had that thought come from? Her damn independent brain was rebelling against her common sense again. She wasn't licking his lip or anything else. *Act like an adult here, Pansy.*

"You've got a—" She pointed to her lip.

Kade scrubbed at his mouth with a napkin before looking at her, his brows raised.

"You got it."

"I look presentable?" When she nodded, he grinned. "Good, now back to the catsuit."

CHAPTER FOUR

Canned music floated through the air-conditioned room and the other patients spoke in hushed tones as Kade waited for his appointment. He hunched down in the plastic chair, ignoring the elderly couple to his left, and got lost in his thoughts again.

In the week since he'd rescued Pansy from the baby shower, he'd wondered what was going through her mind. She'd become increasingly upset as the party wore on. He couldn't imagine the girl he'd known hating babies, but something was going on.

Did she have a child? If so, where was it? Pansy having a baby with someone else killed him. Had she been married? Curiosity was eating him up, but the only way to find out the truth was to ask her.

No way was he doing that. She'd made it clear she wasn't ready to confide in him. Most of the time, she didn't want to talk to him about the weather.

He'd dropped hints to Millie and Wanda Lu, but neither of them knew anything about Pansy's past. Cary had warned him several times to stay away from her friend. Micah's wife wasn't going to offer any information.

"Kade Vaughn?" The nurse waited as he walked across

the room.

He'd only been in Portland for four hours but he was more than ready to get out of the big city. After his two remaining doctor appointments, the only time he'd have to come here would be for a bull riding.

He entered the small examining room and sat in a hard plastic chair. The pretty dark-haired nurse took his blood pressure and temperature and all the things nurses did while you waited for the doc. "Doctor will be with you in a minute." She smiled then disappeared out the door.

Kade pulled out his phone. In his experience with doctors, their minute was about equal to his hour. To his surprise, Dr. Porter arrived before he could check all his emails.

"Hey, Doc." Kade climbed onto the examination table and waited while the doctor looked him over.

"Any headaches, dizziness or nausea?"

"Nope. I feel really good, Doc." No way was he going to tell this guy about the minor headache that was present whenever he got too tired. Or, the occasional bout of the dizzies. "I think I'm ready to start riding. How soon can I enter?"

Dr. Porter shook his head as he took a seat on the stool beside Kade. "Not yet. You've got to give this concussion time to heal. In my opinion, you should hang up your bull rope, but I've taken care of enough rodeo athletes to know that advice falls on deaf ears. Give it three more months."

Three months might as well be three decades. At twenty-nine, he was one of the old timers of bull riding. If he waited another ninety days the finals would be over. He'd done a pretty good job of keeping positive during his rehab, but the doctor's prognosis was depressing.

Chewie's place was about an hour east of Portland.

Kade's plan had been to have dinner and a few beers and shoot the shit with his buddy. He'd even told Micah he was spending the night. After hearing he wasn't released to ride, he couldn't stand the thought of rehashing old bull riding stories, so he drove straight back to East Hope.

As he turned on to Main Street, there sat the Five and Diner right where it had been since sometime in the fifties.

Kade parked in the small lot to the side of the building. Should he go in or not? The last two times he'd dropped by to eat, Pansy had busied herself with customers, ignoring his attempts at conversation.

Well, hell! Nearly everyone he'd ever known had called him hardheaded. Might as well live up to his reputation. As he pulled open the heavy glass door to the café, the enticing smell of fresh coffee greeted him.

Pansy stood with her back to him, chatting with one of the locals. He hesitated, taking a moment to soak in her familiar beauty, before crossing the room to stand behind her and wait for her to finish her conversation.

As she turned, she let out a shriek and almost dropped the pot of coffee she held. "Quit sneaking up on me. You scared me to death," she said, exasperation raising the tone of her voice. She pushed past him, ignoring all the staring customers and hurried to the kitchen.

When Kade made his way through the swinging door, Pansy stood with her arms folded over her chest. He knew she was mad, but took a moment to admire the view. The woman was magnificent.

She was sexy as hell in a short, red gingham dress. The dark wig was pulled into pigtails. Gilligan's Island had never been his favorite show, but Pansy as MaryAnn was enough to get him to rethink his choices.

"Another good choice," Kade said, mimicking her posture. "You've been ignoring me."

"You're not important enough for me to ignore." She turned to the stove and slapped down three hamburger patties. The last one hit the grill, breaking into pieces with the force.

"What happened at the party last week? You were really upset." Kade leaned against the wall and watched her work. If she didn't settle down, she'd have to mix the broken burgers with gravy and serve them over biscuits.

Pansy's shoulders lifted then dropped as a big sigh escaped. "This is really none of your business."

"Something about the baby presents or the party upset you. If you talk about it, maybe you'll feel better." For some reason, Pansy being sad about a baby caused a lump the size of Texas to form in his throat.

She braced her hands on the counter and dropped her head. After a silence filled moment, she turned. Her face was frozen into an implacable frown. "I was pregnant. I lost my baby. Are you happy now, because I don't feel any better."

Sometimes he wondered if his older sister hadn't been right when she'd called him an *idjit* all those years. He'd known something like this was coming, but how was he supposed to make things better? Closing the distance between them, he pulled Pansy into his arms.

She stiffened for a moment then relaxed the slightest bit. Laying her head on his shoulder, she sighed. "I'm done telling you my secrets."

A sudden thought made his breath seize in his lungs. He pushed her away until he could see her eyes. "There's no chance this was our baby is there?"

Her gaze dropped to the floor. When she looked up, her pale blue eyes stared into his. "This baby had nothing to do with us." She tried to wiggle out of his grasp, but he held her tight.

A rush of relief was smothered with a wave of regret. Kade rested his chin on the top of her head. When he'd thought of Pansy through the years, he hadn't thought of her with someone else. He hadn't considered that while he'd gotten along with his life, she'd gotten along with hers. "Where is your husb—?"

The smell of burning meat brought them to their senses. Pansy whirled out of his arms and grabbed the metal spatula. "Double dip dammit!" She scooped up the ruined burgers and dropped them onto a paper plate.

Kade hid a grin when he took the plate from her hands. He'd never heard anyone except Pansy use that particular swear word.

In swift efficient movements, she dropped three more burgers on the grill. "Do you have a dog?"

The opportunity to find out more about Pansy was gone. "I'll take it to Willa's new puppy. She's got so many dogs now, it's going to break Micah buying dog food."

Pansy flipped the burgers. She buttered the buns and placed them on the grill before turning to him. Hands on her hips, she stared at him for several minutes. "Why are you following me around, digging into my personal life?"

"I'm a naturally friendly guy?" Kade could usually use humor to distract people. It hadn't ever worked on the old version of Pansy, and it wasn't working on this new one. He had to quit thinking of her as the girl she'd been. This woman was different, stronger more determined.

She shook her head and waited.

He stared out the tiny window by the door to gather his thoughts. When he looked at Pansy again, her expression had softened. He could pressure her, get her to tell him her secrets, but he was pretty sure she'd run, and he wasn't done with her yet. He settled for, "I like you."

"You don't know me." The stubborn look was back, and the softness she'd shown earlier had gone. She turned, scooped the burgers onto the buns and started putting on the condiments. With lettuce, onion, tomato, cheese, bacon and avocado, the stack was close to tipping over. She put the top buns on and jammed a long toothpick through each one. Fries filled up one plate and potato salad the other two. "I have to go back to work. You can leave through the back door.

When Pansy disappeared through the door to the café, happiness followed along in her wake. Riding bulls was what he did, who he was, and he wasn't ready to change that, but it was getting harder each time he thought of leaving Pansy to go back on the road.

He heard her soft voice through the pass through. "Here you go, Byron. Double order of bacon burgers with salad. Did you want salsa with that?"

Kade watched her chat with her customers. She was friendly to everyone but him. He knew he'd hurt her before, but was it bad enough for her to still be upset? And where had she been the last seven years?

Pansy wasn't about to open up. Her friend, Cary, had shut him down the last time he'd asked. Maybe if he appealed to Cary's sweet side, she'd be more forthcoming, and if he could get Micah to run interference, he might actually live.

~*~

The *Bad To The Bone* ringtone of Pansy's cellphone startled her out of the dream. She hadn't had this fantasy for several years, and had almost forgotten the sense of loss it left behind. She'd been in Kade's arms. Not the Kade she knew now, the Kade she'd thought loved her. In confusion, she glanced around her bedroom.

Just like always, he wasn't there.

Five fifteen glowed in green letters from the front of her phone, and Micah's name was in the caller ID.

"I brought Cary to the hospital late last night. She made me promise to call you." Micah's voice sounded strained. """It's a boy. A big boy."

"Congratulations! How's Cary?" Pansy sat up, pulling the duvet around her shoulders. "The baby's okay, right? Are you in Burns? Where's Willa?"

"Millie and Clinton took Willa home with them." Micah's voice was filled worry and weariness. "The baby's fine. Kade is on his way to pick you up. I'll fill you in on the rest when you get here."

"Wait, what? I don't need him to drive me." Cary pushed her way through the clothes in her closet searching for something to wear. She grabbed an oversized cream sweater and threw it on the bed. "I'm capable of driving myself."

"He's already on his way. I gotta go."

Micah was gone before she could say another word. Damn, now she'd have to put on a wig. She stopped, glancing in the mirror on her antique dressing table. Her long brown hair hung past her shoulders in soft waves.

A more appealing option was to give up on this charade. Hiding behind the alternate personalities had proved useful for a while, but for the first time in years, she didn't feel the need to be someone else. She pulled the sweater over her head and dug through the back of her closet. Folded in a box of old clothes she'd forgotten to give away were a pair of faded Cruel Girl jeans.

Pansy hadn't worn western clothes since she'd left home. Slipping into them, she was surprised to find the waist a little baggy. Stress wasn't the best diet plan, but she had't had much choice.

She padded into the kitchen and started a pot of coffee brewing then sat on the wooden stool by the pantry and pulled on one red cowboy boot then the other. Popping the lid off her travel mug, she filled it with the dark, rich liquid and a healthy dose of cream. At least she could meet Kade adequately caffeinated.

The sound of his knock brought her to her feet. "Come on in." She grabbed her coat and hurried to the living room.

Kade's gaze traveled over her then he met her eyes. "Who are you channeling today?"

She straightened then walked past him, her head held high. She might not be in costume, but she could embrace the other women's strength. "We'll talk about it in the truck."

He didn't speak for the first fifteen miles of the trip, and although that's what Pansy had hoped for, it was becoming uncomfortable. "Want to talk?"

His head turned slowly until their eyes met, then he fixed his eyes back on the road. "No costumes? Why?"

Pansy stared out the window. He'd recognized her soon after they'd met at the café; there never had been a chance to fool him. But it had been easier to ignore the truth than to explain. "I decided it was time to come to terms with my past."

Kade cleared his throat. He drummed his fingers on the steering wheel. "I was beginning to wonder—"

The headlights illuminated the brush and juniper along the sides of the road. Kade slowed when a doe and fawn walked to the edge of the road before melting back into the desert night.

Moonlight brightened the interior of the truck enough for Pansy to see the man she'd given her heart to so long ago.

He turned his piercing gray eyes on her for a moment before shifting his attention to the up-coming curve.

Pansy took a deep breath. Time to fess up. "It was pretty obvious who you were when Micah introduced us. I just didn't want to deal with our past." The tips of her fingers felt like ice, and she couldn't seem to pull a full breath into her lungs. She'd spent seven years getting every last bit of tension out of her life. Now within a couple of weeks, she was drowning in drama.

Technically, Kade chuckled, but there was no humor in the sound, and he didn't bother to comment.

When she realized he wasn't going to speak, she continued. "I don't know what else to say." This conversation would be easier if she had room to pace. She twisted the turquoise ring on her index finger in agitation. "I didn't think I'd ever see you again."

"I looked for you."

She snorted. "Not very hard. I tried to call you, but you let it go to voice-mail. I waited, but you didn't call back."

"You're right, I should have returned your calls. I wasn't ready to have the same argument again. After our last big blow-up, I gave up. But when I did come home, I looked for you."

"You came home after how long?"

"I don't know. A while."

"More like two years." Pansy jerked her head up and glared. "You were gone for two years."

"But then I looked everywhere. I even talked to your dad." Kade's brows drew together into a frown. "He said he didn't have a daughter."

"That's what he told me, too." Pansy dropped her head back against the headrest and closed her eyes. Her sigh held the weight of all the people who'd let her down. "You were two years too late."

A few lights brightened the windows of the businesses in Burns, but only the occasional car was on the street at this hour. Kade pulled into the parking lot of the abandoned lumber mill at the edge of town. "Where have you been, Pansy?"

Apparently they were going to have this conversation whether she wanted to or not. "All over. Mostly in Denver."

"Why there?" Kade tilted the steering wheel up and twisted in the seat so he faced her. He fished a roll of Peppermint Lifesavers out of the truck's console and offered her one.

Pansy shook her head. Candy wasn't going to make this any easier. "You're just full of questions, aren't you?"

Popping a Lifesaver into his mouth, he waited for her to continue.

"Denver was as good as anyplace. I didn't intend on staying, but I found a job I liked. That's where I met Cary."

"Just one more question. Why the wigs and the costumes?"

Pansy sat back, memories of that time of her life rolling over her like a smothering wave of smoke. She pushed the button to roll down the window. Maybe some fresh air would help.

The need to redefine herself had been uncontrollable, to become someone else essential. "I didn't like who I was or what my life had become so I changed."

"Why did you feel you had to change?"

"Nope, you used your one more question. Let's get to the hospital."

Kade stared at her, his brows pulled down into a frown. Even frowning, the warmth in his gray eyes made her want to…. No!

She straightened her spine and met his gaze, daring him to push her further.

He turned the key and pulled out onto the road without a word. The lights of the hospital glowed ahead of them and not a moment too soon.

A dull headache throbbed behind Pansy's eyes, and there was a slight tremor in her hands. It had been too much to ask that she could have continued to live her life the way she chose, without attachments, without explanation.

Sure it was lonely, but these last few tension filled weeks left her exhausted. "Look, can we not talk about my past. I prefer to live in the present."

Several empty parking spots were near the hospital entrance, and Kade pulled into one. Climbing from the truck, he started toward the large glass doors at the entrance. Halfway to the building, he stopped and stood staring at his boots. After a moment, he turned to face her. "I've missed you, Pansy."

CHAPTER FIVE

Not looking back to see if Pansy followed, Kade strode through the halls of the hospital. It's not like she could get lost in this small building, and she'd done well enough on her own all these years. She hadn't needed him at all.

Why he'd thought she might this time around he didn't know. All this time he'd wondered how she was doing. It had occurred to him she might have found another love, but call him stupid, he hadn't taken the idea seriously. Not really.

Through the years, when he'd shaken out his memories of Pansy, he'd preferred to think of her waiting for him, even though he'd known she wasn't.

Sometimes he was a corn-fed idiot!

He was rounding the corner next to the surgery suite when a hand grabbed his arm.

Pansy stood, fingers warm against his skin, with a frown on her face. "So let me get this straight. You're mad because I didn't jump up and down, excited to be seeing you again, when Micah introduced us, but it's okay that you didn't tell me you recognized me? What kind of crap is that?" The scuffed toe of her old red boot tapped the floor in irritation, and her fingernails skimmed across his skin as she pulled her hand away.

Kade stepped into an empty waiting room and pulled Pansy with him. The soft blues and browns of the upholstery and paint were designed to sooth, and he needed all the tranquility he could find.

When he turned to her, the sight of the woman he'd known took his breath away. Pansy in the café was eye-catching, but without the costumes, wigs and make-up, she was the prettiest woman he'd ever seen. He raised his hand to touch her cheek, but decided that wouldn't be a smart move. Walking to a row of chairs, he sat down, waiting until she joined him.

"I'm not mad. I don't know what I am, but the sight of you, the real you, scrambled what little brain I have left." He reached for her hand, hesitated, then picked it up. The skin of her palm was a soft contrast to his calluses. "You haven't changed."

"Everything about me has changed." Her tone was abrupt, but there was a slight hitch to her voice as she freed her hand from his grasp. "I'm not the girl you knew."

If he didn't move away, he'd keep touching her, and he couldn't think when his fingers came in contact with her soft skin. The water cooler in the corner of the room gurgled, and Kade had a sudden desire for a drink. The cool water didn't help much with the fire that burned inside him, but getting a drink bought him time to think. He lifted the paper cup to his lips, watching her over the edge. "I'm sorry I hurt you."

"You have no idea." The words came out so quiet he almost didn't hear. She walked to the window and when she spoke again, her voice was strong. "That was a long time ago. Forget it happened. I have."

"You said you lost a baby. When was that?" It couldn't be his. She'd said it wasn't, and Pansy wouldn't lie about something that important. Besides, someone from home would have told him. Somehow he would have known.

Pansy waived her hand in dismissal. "Sorry, but that subject is off limits. We came to see how Cary and Micah are doing, and that's what I'm going to do."

Kade stood alone in the doorway, watching Pansy stride down the hall. Filled with more questions than he'd had before, he had no choice but to follow her. He'd been amused when he'd first seen her dressed as Cleopatra. He wasn't amused now.

What if he had been the father of Pansy's baby? Was he ready to settle down and live like a normal family? For the first time in his life, bull riding wasn't at the forefront of his thoughts. He wasn't ready to retire—was he? He'd found fame and a little fortune as a rodeo cowboy.

But without a bull riding championship, he was just another nobody.

As Kade entered the maternity waiting room, his problems melted away the moment he saw Micah grab Pansy and pull her into a hug. The skin of his friend's face was gray and drawn, his eyes bloodshot.

Micah let Pansy lead him to a group of chairs.

"I don't like the looks of this. What happened?" Kade moved closer to his friend but remained standing.

"Man, I was so scared. Cary had trouble having the baby, and the doctor did an emergency Cesarean."

"But she's okay? The baby's okay?" Kade hadn't known Micah's wife long, but after years of misery and deception by his ex-wife, Cary had found a way to make his cousin happy. That counted for a lot.

Micah started to answer, but had to clear his throat. "The baby's fine, but Cary kept bleeding. They gave her a transfusion. They might have to give her another."

"Tell me they got the bleeding stopped." Pansy blinked back tears and cleared her throat. Micah didn't need to see either of them fall apart.

"For now, but they're having trouble getting her blood pressure to stabilize."

"Oh, Micah," Pansy took Micah's hand and held it

between her own.

Micah nodded. "The doctors said barring complications she'd make a full recovery. It's the complications part that bothers me."

The look on his face confirmed he wasn't sure he believed the medical personnel. "If they told you Cary's going to be fine, she'll be fine. Doctors don't lie about things like this."

Something in the tone of Pansy's voice told Kade she was speaking from experience.

Micah leaned back in the chair and rubbed his face with his hands. "I can't lose her."

The desolation on his friend's expression broke Kade's heart. What did you say in a situation like this? No use telling him not to worry. That wasn't going to happen. No good saying she'd be okay when they weren't sure. "Want a cup of coffee?" At least that would give him something to do.

Eyes closed, Micah only shrugged.

Pansy glanced at him then looked away, swiping at a tear. "I think coffee would do us all good."

The next hour dragged along with Pansy trying to keep a conversation going. They'd run out of the smallest of small talk when they heard a high-pitched voice coming from the hall.

"Shit, I forgot to call Clinton. He and Millie are bringing Willa to meet her little brother." Micah dropped his head into his hands, giving in to exhaustion. "I don't want her to worry."

"Pansy, you stay with Micah. I'll cut them off." He hurried to the doorway and caught the group before they saw Micah. "Hey, Willa Wild. Let's go see your brother. He's in the nursery.

Clinton looked at him, his brows drawn down in confusion.

Kade gave his head a small shake and took the little girl's hand in one of his, and Millie's in the other. "Big sisters can see their new brother this way."

Willa Wild broke free and skipped back down the hall.

"What's going on?" Millie asked, her voice just above a whisper.

Kade stopped. "There were some complications, but I think Cary is going to be okay. Micah, on the other hand, I'm not so sure about. I think we need to keep Willa with us for awhile."

Clinton put his arm around Millie's shoulder and pulled her close. "Show us the way. We'll take her out for ice cream later if we need to."

Millie nodded her assent, and they followed Kade to the nursery.

Willa vibrated with excitement at the prospect of being a first-time big sister. Bouncing like Tigger, she tried to get high enough to see through the large window. "I can't see him. Can you see him? I want to see him."

Kade lifted her—she weighed less than a bucket of grain—and they looked through the glass together, trying to read the name cards attached to the beds. It wasn't necessary. There were only five babies in the nursery. Four were wrapped in pink.

"There he is." Kade pointed at the tiny bundle in blue.

Willa lifted her small hand and waved to her brother then leaned in until her turned-up nose was squashed against the glass. "Hi, Rodie."

Kade looked at the little girl, a smile finally working its way out. "Rodie?"

Willa's carrot red hair floated around her head as the grin, missing two teeth, lit her face. "Yes. Rodie Owen West. I picked out the name myself. Well, Pa helped."

"Rodie Owen?" He gave Willa Wild a high five then a low five. "Good job, girl."

"How soon do you think I'll get to hold him?" Willa turned back to look through the window. She raised her hand and placed the palm against the glass.

A nurse from inside waved to them then picked up

Rodie and held him closer to the window. The baby opened his eyes for a moment then yawned.

"He looked at me. He knows me." Willa's voice was filled with awe.

"Looks like he's tired from being born," Millie said. "How about if we go to the Dairy Queen for a blizzard to celebrate?"

"Can I see Cary?" Willa looked into Kade's eyes then she wiggled trying to get down.

"She's resting, Willa. It's hard work having a baby." Kade put the little girl on her feet.

"Uncle Kade, you know my name is Willa Wild." After he nodded, she took Millie's hand. "Can I have a sundae?"

Millie looked from Kade to Clinton then back to the little girl, a forced smile on her face. "Sure, you can have anything you want. We're celebrating the day you became a big sister."

"That's an important day for sure." Clinton took Willa's other hand, and they walked to the elevator. The last thing Kade heard was Willa telling Clinton and Millie how she was going to teach Rodie to ride her horse.

As the elevator doors slid shut, he turned to go back to the waiting room. Moving along the hushed hallway, he passed the chapel and for some unknown reason, stepped inside. He'd never been on close speaking terms with the big guy. Hell, he hadn't give God much thought for years, but it couldn't hurt to ask, could it?

After a short, and he hoped good-enough prayer, Kade hurried back to Micah. Let there be good news, or at least, not bad.

~*~

The first twelve hours after the baby was born crawled by like a hobbled sloth. Pansy's worry for Cary increased with each passing minute until her muscles were rigid with tension and fear. For the first time in years, she'd found someone she trusted, and now she was in danger of losing her friend.

She heard muffled footsteps coming down the hall and jumped to her feet when Micah entered the waiting room, bracing for bad news.

"Dr. Carter just finished examining Cary. They've stabilized her, thank god."

Pansy hadn't been a demonstrative person for years. She'd kept to herself, not getting attached to anyone, but now she pulled Micah into a gigantic hug. If the waiting had been bad for her, it must have been excruciating for him. She tried to say something, but her throat was full of tears and thankfulness, so she hugged him again.

"Cary's is going to have to stay in the hospital for a few days." Micah dropped into a chair, stretching his long legs out in front of him and his arms over his head. "God, I'm glad that's over. I thought I was going to lose her."

Pansy sat beside him, leaning down to make eye contact. "But we didn't lose her. She's going to be fine."

"Now I have to figure out what to do with my Willa." Micah sat, his forearms on his thighs, his head hanging, a position she'd seen the man in far too often since this started. "Millie and Clinton would take her, but they both have jobs to do."

"We'll handle it." Kade sat up from where he'd been sleeping on the floor. "You stay here with Cary, and we'll take Willa home."

"I can't ask you—"

"You didn't ask. I offered." Kade stood and poured himself a cup of coffee. "Pansy'll help me out."

Pansy instinctively shook her head no. The way her throat constricted when Kade volunteered them for babysitting duty made it impossible to swallow. Since she'd lost Maxie she'd kept as far away from children as she could. It was too painful.

She pulled in a deep breath and gave herself a mental talking to. Now was not the time to give in to her fears.

"Count me in. It'll be fun." It would be fun in a pain-filled, break-your-heart kind of way.

At least her voice didn't convey her true feelings.

Micah raised his head, his eyes red-rimmed, but he apparently bought her story. "Thank you."

Pansy waved her hand in a nonchalant manner, the exact opposite of the panic raging through her at the thought of being responsible for an eight-year-old. "Pffft! Kade and I can take care of one little girl. No problem."

Micah quirked an eyebrow, no doubt worrying about the way she and Kade would take care of his daughter.

Kade laughed. "How hard can it be? She's just a little girl."

Micah shook his head. "My daughter could sweet talk Putin into giving up the Russian presidency. Did she tell you what she named the baby?"

"Rodie? How'd she come up with that?"

"Cary and I had almost settled on Carter Rodie. Rodie was my mom's maiden name." His laugh was soft. "Like we'd have the last say."

"It was nice of you to let Willa have a hand in naming her brother," Pansy said.

"She knew my dad's name was Owen. She insisted the baby be named after him." Placing his hands on the small of his back, he stretched with a groan. "When Cary and I got our first glimpse of Rodie, the name seemed to fit. Besides, how can you beat the name Rodie Owen West for a little cowboy?"

Kade moved around Micah to stand beside Pansy. He placed his arm around her shoulder like they were friends or something. She thought about moving away, but it felt nice. She could always tell him off later.

"Let's get on down the road. Millie and Clinton will be waiting for us."

Micah reached for his wallet. "You'll need money for groceries or something."

Kade took Pansy's hand and pulled her toward the

hallway. "We don't need your stinkin' money." With a wave, he trotted down the hall, dragging her behind him.

After a short stop at the Burns Grocery, the ride back to the ranch passed mostly in silence. Clinton's truck was parked in front of the porch, and they could see Willa on her horse in the corral. Millie watched from the fence while Clinton helped the girl.

Pansy climbed out of the truck and leaned against the fender. The scene reminded her of her childhood, if you ignored the fact that, unlike her father, Clinton was patient and easy going. What would it be like to learn something without your dad yelling at you? That was something she'd never know.

Kade slumped against the truck beside her, his smile even bigger if that was possible. "It's almost dinner time. I'm going to go wrangle that little cowgirl. You get the grub ready." His deep voice sent shivers down her spine.

"There you go, slipping back into vintage western movie dialogue. This is the twenty-first century, you know." She slipped her traitorous fingers into the pockets of her jeans before they could grasp the front of Kade's shirt and pull him into her arms.

"If I remember right, you don't like cussing. This way I don't cuss."

"You don't cuss anymore? Because I remember you swore like a sailor." Pansy felt her shoulders relaxing as she chatted with Kade. "You knew so many bad words the Journalism professor gave you an A on your poem."

"That class was hard."

"You thought it would be easy. I'd hoped I'd finally found something I was better at than you." She walked to the porch steps and went up halfway. "Then the teacher gave you an A for originality."

If Kade was trying to look shocked and insulted, he failed. The laughter in his eyes gave him away. "Not true. And I didn't say I didn't cuss anymore. I'm trying to not cuss around you."

His charm was in full bloom, and, like an idiot, Pansy realized she was falling into his trap. He'd always had a way of getting her to relax. And she'd let her guard down. "You don't need to do anything for me. Just take care of Willa."

Kade's smile faded. He stared into her eyes for a moment then shrugged and walked toward the barn.

Why did life have to be so hard? Why couldn't Kade have loved her enough to stay with her back then? Why couldn't their baby have lived? Why…

Enough of the wallowing! The past couple of years, she'd come to terms with losing Maxie. She'd managed to get rid of all the hassle, until the cowboy waltzed into her life again. Time to get back to her original plan.

Filling her arms with groceries, she made several trips to get the food into the house. A note taped to the refrigerator mentioned three casseroles in the freezer and a fresh cherry pie in the pantry. Pansy was a master of BBQ and all things meat, but Cary was an angel with pastries of any kind. Her pies were legendary.

"After the day we've had, we need fresh food." She unwrapped the chicken breasts they'd bought and set about making one of her favorites. She was sliding the roaster into the oven when Kade and little Willa entered the kitchen followed by Millie.

"Where's Clinton?" Pansy pulled a bag of fresh green beans from the fridge and started snapping the ends off. The smell of bacon bits popping and frying made her mouth water. "I'll have dinner ready in a little bit."

"Oh, honey. He's feeding the livestock then we have to be going." Millie scooped the bacon onto a paper towel to drain. "Are you sure you don't need us to bring you anything?"

Pansy dumped the bean ends into the trash. She pulled the small steamer from one of the lower cabinets and filled it with water. "No, we picked up groceries today on the way home. Thanks anyway."

Millie turned to Kade. "Did Clinton tell you what needs to be done around here while Micah's gone?"

"Yeah, we got it all worked out. He's taking care of the ranch, and I'm doing the chores here at home, and watching out for Miss Willa Wild." Kade grinned at the little girl.

Her high-pitched giggle filled the room as she snitched a bit of bacon.

What had started out this morning as a cute bun on the top of Willa's head had slipped to just above her right ear. Curly red tendrils that had escaped the rainbow colored Scrunchie framed her elfin face.

As Millie talked, she pulled out the band and redid the little girl's hairdo. "That's better. Give Aunt Millie a hug good-bye."

Kade and Willa walked the older woman out.

Before Pansy had the cheese grated, Kade reappeared. "How long until we eat?"

"Thirty minutes." Pansy dropped the beans into the steamer, adding the bacon bits and a few spices. "Where's Willa?"

"Saying good-bye to Clinton. She'll be in in a minute." Kade looked into the pot then fished out a piece of bacon with a fork. "Neither Millie or Clinton have kids of their own. They make the perfect grandparents for a little girl who needs some."

They would have been perfect for Pansy's daughter if she'd lived, too. She shook off the depressing thought. Living with *What ifs* just made her crazy. "Do you want a beer while we wait?" Pansy opened the refrigerator and pulled out two bottles of Coors Original. "I haven't had one of these in years."

"You used to drink them with me." Kade waggled his eyebrows

Keeping the past in the past was hard with Kade here reminding her how good life had been for a while. "A lot of things changed when you left, including my choice of drinks.”

CHAPTER SIX

One thing about this new Pansy, the woman was a hell of a cook.

In the years they'd dated, she'd made some quick meals, but never ventured out of casseroles and sandwiches. Last night's dinner, chicken breasts stuffed with cheese, baked potatoes and fresh beans, was one of Kade's new, all-time favorite meal. Make that his all-time favorite dinner, because the cranberry pancakes topped with whipped cream that she'd made this morning was his new favorite breakfast. If she kept this up, he'd weigh as much as the bulls he rode.

"Willa wants to learn to barrel race, and I was telling her you were one of the best college barrel racers in Montana. Want to help?" Kade wondered if she still rode. The whole time he'd known her, a day hadn't gone by that she hadn't been with her horses.

"I haven't been on a horse in years." Pansy suddenly became interested in loading the dishwasher. "And I have things to do in here."

Willa dragged a chair toward the sink, the legs screeching across the hardwood. "I'll help clean the dishes, and then you can come with us." She climbed on the chair and held out her hands. "I'll put the glasses in the cupboard."

Pansy looked at Kade, apprehension in her eyes. "I gave up everything to do with rodeo when I left home. I see no reason to start up again."

"You have to come see my new horse." Willa waited, one arm outstretched. "Hand me a glass, please."

The moment Pansy gave up and agreed to come with them, Kade relaxed a little. It was obvious she didn't want to ride, but she wouldn't hurt Willa's feelings for the world. One of these days, he'd get her to tell him the truth of her past, but until then, he'd be patient. "I'll get started saddling."

Kade grabbed a rope halter off the hook by the pen and slipped it on Rondo. Of all the horses on the Circle W, the black gelding was his favorite. As he brushed the sleek animal, questions ran through his mind. Could it be Pansy really didn't want to ride? That was so unlike her, he wondered if something else was going on.

Before, Pansy had lived for her horses. How could her love of them change so completely?

He heard Willa Wild long before the girls got to the barn. In her high-pitched voice, she was explaining to Pansy about her new horse.

"I used to have a pony, but I got too big. We sent him to a little kid. Two Bits is just my size, and he's the smartest horse on the ranch. Clinton says so." The tiny redhead skipped into the barn aisle, pulling on Pansy's hand. Her voice raised by two octaves when she saw Kade. "You didn't catch Two Bits for me, did you? I can do it myself."

Kade was pretty sure there was nothing in this world Willa Wild couldn't do if she set her mind to it. "No, he's in his pen. Your halter is over there." He pointed to the bright pink bundle on the bench by the tack room.

Willa grabbed the halter and, with the lead rope dragging along behind her kicking up little puffs of dust, she ran toward the pen outside.

"Is she okay by herself with the horse?" Pansy started to follow the girl.

"She could probably use some help buckling the halter." He looked up to meet her eyes. For a moment, he thought he saw the private, loving look she'd used to give him, but it disappeared quickly. He cleared his throat. "She usually just throws the lead rope over Two Bits' neck, and he follows her."

Pansy turned away, but not before Kade saw a genuine smile. He'd missed that smile, so he tried again. "I think she's right. Two Bits is the bestest horse ever born."

It worked. A wide grin spread across Pansy's face at Kade's imitation of Willa. Her grin grew wider as she watched the girl lead in a small brown horse.

"Isn't he pretty?" As Willa reached up, Two Bits lowered his head to the girl's level. She traced the small white spot on his forehead.

In the world of show horses, Two Bit's legs were a little too short and his head was a lot too big, but here looks weren't everything . . . or anything, really. "The prettiest," Pansy said as she fastened the halter.

"Brush him and I'll get your saddle." Kade swung his saddle onto Rondo's back and reached under the animal to snag the cinch.

Willa turned toward him, her hands on her hips, a frown on her face. "You know I don't ride with a saddle. I'm an Indian Princess."

Kade couldn't stop the laugh that bubbled out of his chest. "Okay, Indian Princess. I thought we'd have Pansy teach you how to barrel race today, but if you want to ride bareback, we'll just go ride down by the creek." He grabbed a halter, disappeared into the corner stall then led out a pretty roan.

"Wait!" Willa Wild drew the short word out into three long syllables. She turned to Pansy, throwing out her arms. "You can teach me to run barrels?"

~*~

Pansy stiffened. "I haven't done that in years, honey. I won't be a very good teacher."

Kade knew barrel racing had been Pansy's passion since she'd been big enough to hold the reins by herself. She'd poured every waking minute into learning to be the best. Something had changed, and it wasn't for the better.

She turned to him. "You'd better find someone else."

"Please, please, please." Willa stood in front of Pansy, jumping up and down, her cheeks flushed. "I want to be a barrel racer just like Sherry Cervi."

"She's only going to walk around the barrels." Kade watched the conflicting emotions playing out across Pansy's face.

"This is my lifelong dream." The look on the eight-year-old's face was priceless along side her words.

"Lifelong?" Kade couldn't help but ask.

The serious blue eyes glared at him. "Yes. Since I was six." Willa Wild turned back to Pansy. "Pretty please, Pansy."

Pansy would be a tougher person than he was if she could say no to this little girl. Micah's warning in the hospital had been dead on. In a few years, Willa Wild was going to run some poor guy ragged.

"Okay," Pansy said with a sigh. "Just for today."

Kade got the tiny saddle from the tack room then straightened the blanket Willa Wild had somehow thrown across Two Bits' back. He snugged the cinch and tried to lift the little girl onto her horse. "Go warm up Two Bits."

"I need my horse's boots first. We can't have him hurting his legs. All the good barrel racers use boots." Willa Wild slid down and hurried into the tack room. She came back with a set of four turquoise boots. "I can put them on by myself."

Kade suspected the boots weren't technically on right,

but he wasn't an expert. If one ended up on each leg, that would be good enough for today.

"Where's your bridle?" Pansy asked, starting toward the tack room.

"Two Bits is so well trained, I ride him in a halter."

Kade saddled the roan, watching Pansy interact with Willa. They stood, heads together, combing the tangles out of Two Bits' mane. Pansy looked at him and his heart gave a weird thump. The two made a pretty picture, but he noticed the tension in Pansy's body despite her smile.

"Is that true? About the halter?" she asked.

Kade adjusted the stirrups on the roan's saddle. "Yup. Two Bits is the best trained horse in Oregon."

Pansy moved back to Willa Wild. "Need a boost?"

Exasperation filled the little girl's expression. "Pansy, I can do this myself. Tell her, Kade." She led Two Bits to the fence. The horse dropped his head and cocked a hip, waiting while his rider climbed the rails and jumped onto his back. "Aren't you ready yet?"

Kade slipped a bridle on the roan gelding before dropping the reins into Pansy's hand. "Ready?" He slid the snaffle bit into Rondo's mouth and followed Willa toward the door.

"Wait! I didn't say I was going to ride." Pansy jogged after them. She stuffed the reins toward Kade.

Turning his back on her, he put his foot into the stirrup and mounted. As he rode away, he looked back over his shoulder. "Just lead Smog around then. He needs the exercise. Come on, Willa Wild. Let's ride."

Willa kicked her horse into a slow jog, her wild, curly-red hair dancing around her face. "Look at me!" Her joyful, little-girl voice rang across the arena.

How could anyone be in a bad mood around this child? She radiated happiness. He turned to share the moment with Pansy, just to see her standing where he'd left her, looking at Smog.

She reached out a tentative hand and stroked the

gelding's nose then wrapped her arms around his neck and buried her face in his shiny, black mane. Her love for horses had apparently overcome whatever misgivings she had about riding. She looked up to see Kade watching her and gave him a sad smile. "Nice horse."

Kade pretended to ignore her melancholy. "Micah bought him for Cary to learn to barrel race on just before she became pregnant. Climb aboard."

Pansy mounted with the grace of someone who'd ridden most of her life. She turned to Kade. "I'll just sit on him."

~*~

Swinging a leg over a horse for the first time in seven years felt like coming home. The things Pansy had missed most, besides Kade, were her horses, but when she'd left home, she'd put all things rodeo from her mind. It was just too painful to dwell on what she'd lost.

When her father had given her the choice of an abortion or leaving, she'd damn near knocked him over on the way out. She'd spent months agonizing, but no matter how she looked at it, she hadn't been able to figure out a way to support her horses on her own.

The only good point she could remember about her dad was that he loved animals and his God above all else—people, not so much, and his wayward daughter, apparently, not at all.

When she touched her heels to his sides, Smog moved out smoothly. He responded to her cues without hesitation. She felt a small smile form on her lips. She hadn't forgotten at all how much she enjoyed riding. To keep from going crazy those first terrible years after Kade left, she'd hidden all desire to rodeo from herself by becoming a city girl.

"This is a nice horse." She rode over to where Kade was watching them. "But his name has to go. Who came up with Smog?"

"I know this will come as a surprise, but Willa named him, and Cary didn't have the heart to tell her no." He eased Rondo into a lope and warmed the horse up.

Pansy reached down and checked the knot where Willa's lead rope was tied to the halter. "Are you sure you don't need a bridle?" she asked the little girl.

"Two Bits doesn't like a bridle very well. We like this better."

"Woohoo, Willa Wild! Bet I can outrun you and Two Bits." Kade loped his horse up to them and stopped. "Let's have a race. Time us, Pansy."

"I don't have a stop watch."

Willa looked from her to Kade and shook her head. Apparently, that was a dumb thing to say, but Willa was too polite to call her on it. "You just count. You know, one, two, three until we finish."

"I get to go first." Kade sent a friendly challenge to his small opponent.

"No, I do." Willa practically vibrated with excitement.

Kade put his fingertips to his forehead. "How do we decide? I know." He pointed to the girl. "Pick a number between one and ten. Highest number wins."

Willa leaned forward and wrapped her arms around her horse's neck as far as they'd go while she thought. She sat up with a smile. "Two for two bits."

Kade's shoulders fell in mock disappointment. "You win. My number was one."

Watching the interaction between the two, Pansy realized he really enjoyed this little girl. His pleasure wasn't an act, and it was obvious Willa adored Kade.

Her breathing hitched, and she swallowed hard. He would have made a great daddy. She struggled to contain the tears that were threatening to spill. Pretending to check Smog's cinch, she turned away from the other two. If Kade hadn't wanted to be a bull rider more than he'd wanted her, and if Maxie had lived, this could be her family. If, if, if…

Playing the *If game* got you nothing but heartache.

"I'm ready Pansy. Tell me to go." Willa Wild's high-pitched voice called to her, reinforcing her feeling of loss.

Pansy wiped at her eyes with her sleeve and took a deep breath. The last thing she needed was for Kade to see her fall apart.

"What's wrong?"

Double dip damn! Kade's voice sent shivers down her spine. No matter her feelings, her traitorous body still reacted whenever he got close to her.

Pansy gave the latigo one last tug and turned to him. "Where's the starting line?"

The look he gave her said he knew she was upset. "Are you okay?"

She waved a hand at him, shooing away his concern. "I'm fine, but you'd better get your game face on or that little redhead over there is going to whip your butt." She swung aboard Smog and trotted over to Willa.

It felt good to be back in the saddle again. The pretty bay roan moved with athletic ease, his trot smooth and slow. Pansy nudged the horse with her heels and he broke into an easy lope. The feeling of peace she'd always felt when she was around a horse returned full force.

As she came up beside the other horses, Pansy asked Smog to stop. He melted into the ground at her command. "I know I've said this a few times already, but this is a nice horse. Cary's a lucky one."

"She will be when she learns to ride." He reached over and stroked the gelding's neck. "He's going to be a great teacher."

Willa hung off the side of Two Bits then dropped to the ground. She dragged the toe of her boot through the dirt, making a line about twelve inches long. "Here's the starting line. And it will be the finish line, too. Now can we please have our race?"

Kade chuckled. "Are you going to run on foot? Cause I

know I can beat you that way."

Willa Wild raced back to her horse, grabbed the reins and started running toward the fence. Two Bits didn't move, and when Willa hit the end of the reins, she tipped over backwards. "Shoot and shinola!" She climbed to her feet and slapped her jeans. Dust rolled off the fabric and hung in the air.

"Where did you learn that?" Pansy couldn't keep the laughter out of her voice.

Willa looked up, a smudge of dirt across her nose. "Clinton teached me, but I'm not supposed to let my pa hear me say it. You won't tell, will you?"

"I won't tell," Pansy promised.

"Come here." Kade reached down and clasped Willa's hand, hauling her on to his horse. With a touch of the reins, he maneuvered Rondo to stand beside Two Bits and lifted the girl into her saddle. "Now we're ready to rumble."

"Can I go now?" Two Bits did his statue impersonation while his young rider wiggled in the saddle.

"Watch me so you learn the barrel pattern." Pansy loped Smog through the barrels, enjoying the feel of riding a well-trained horse. She stopped by Willa Wild. "Can you do that?"

"Pa showed me." Willa Wild rode her horse to the line, grabbed her saddle horn. She leaned forward. "Tell me when to go."

Pansy heard a snort and turned to see Kade trying unsuccessfully to contain his laughter. "Well, tell her to go," he said when he'd caught his breath.

"Go!"

Willa Wild's short legs pummeled Two Bits' sides, kicking the air more than touching her horse. Her hands flapped with frantic energy while holding the reins. Two Bits took a tentative step forward then broke into a slow trot. "Look at me run," Willa called as she tilted back and forth with each step.

The smile on Willa's face couldn't have been wider as she trotted across the finish line. "How fast was I?" The child was breathing much harder than her horse, but then, Pansy knew she'd worked harder.

"You were twenty. Twenty seconds." Pansy looked at Kade. "You're next."

"You just watch." Kade tipped his cowboy hat at Willa. "I'll show you how this is done."

"You're gonna have to be fast to beat me," the little girl called back.

He rode his horse to the line, lifted his reins as high as he could and yelled, "H-yah, h-yah!" Rondo shifted his weight, looking confused, but didn't move a foot.

Willa Wild's high-pitched laughter filled the arena. "You can't make him go."

Kade frowned at her. "I can too." He bounced in his saddle, shook the reins at Rondo then slumped, a comical scowl on his face. "He won't go."

"You gotta— You gotta— You gotta kick him." Willa Wild was having trouble getting the words out between the giggles.

"That's how I make him go?" Kade turned to Willa Wild. "I just kick?"

The picture of the little cowgirl teaching the big bull rider to ride made Pansy sigh.

"Okay, here we go." He touched his heels to Rondo's sides, and the gelding trotted toward the second barrel.

"Wait, Kade! Wait!" Willa Wild bounced up and down on the small bay horse's back. She waved her arms to get his attention.

Pansy watched Kade stop his horse and walk back to them.

"What now?" He lifted his hands, palm up in question, but he was having a hard time keeping his face straight.

Willa Wild patted him on the shoulder, stretching her small hand out to reach Kade. "You're not very good at this, are you? You're going the wrong way."

CHAPTER SEVEN

For the last three days, at exactly two o'clock in the afternoon, Willa had dragged Pansy and Kade to the barn. And each time, two of the people in the arena had a great time. The other one wavered between having fun and wallowing in misery.

For the life of him, Kade couldn't imagine what had happened to Pansy to cause her wide range of emotions.

Most of the time, pure joy lit on Pansy's face as she watched Willa trot Two Bits through the barrels, but the beautiful expression could turn to pain at a moment's notice.

A wave of guilt raced beneath his skin. If he'd stayed, maybe whatever tragedy she'd weathered wouldn't have happened. Maybe she'd be happy now.

He'd known Pansy Lark better than anyone, or thought he had, but she'd changed. She was harder, more mercurial, a puzzle he couldn't figure out.

Now that Willa had gone to the house with Clinton, it was time to try again. "Something's going on. Want to tell me about it?"

Pansy lugged her saddle into the tack room and lifted it onto the rack. She picked the bridle up off the floor and hung it where it belonged. "I don't know what you mean." Her eyes narrowed and her lips clenched into a thin line, daring him to push her further.

Kade had never been one to back off from a fight. It was time to get this out in the open. "Look, you have fun helping Willa, but whenever I say anything, you look like I've killed your cat. I want to know what I did to deserve this."

Pansy attempted a smile, a smile that didn't work. "That's silly. I never had a cat."

He should keep this light, keep the banter going, but her obvious discomfort whenever she was around him, had him baffled. "You know what I mean. Tell me what's wrong."

"Nothing's wrong. Drop it, please."

He'd run the scenario of their breakup through his mind for hours each night, going over everything that had happened all those years ago.

Was she still this angry with him for leaving? Did she still think they should have gotten married right out of college? Had he hurt her that badly? "I don't know what to do to make this better."

"You never did." Pansy headed for the house.

Kade caught her arm, stopping her in her tracks.

"Let me go." She jerked her arm free. "You gave up the right to know my business seven years ago. As far as I'm concerned, you're someone I met in another life. Nothing more."

Lengthening his stride until he walked beside her, Kade took a moment to think. He hadn't brought up the fight they'd had. Maybe now was the time. "I'm sorry I hurt you. We were kids. We needed to grow up."

She whirled on him. "You certainly helped me do that, whether I was ready or not."

"I said I was sorry. What more do you want?"

"Why are you all-fired determined to get me to tell you every little thing that's gone on in my life since you left?"

Pansy stopped just before the porch. She bent and plucked a clover from the lawn, concentrating as she pulled off each leaf.

"I'm worried about you." Kade leaned against the porch rail, crossing his arms across his chest. "I'm just worried."

"I can take care of myself." Pansy tossed what was left of the clover onto the lawn. "I've been doing it for seven years."

"What do you want me to say?"

Pansy dropped to the step and stretched out her legs. Her smile didn't hide the pain in her eyes. "There's really nothing to say, is there?"

Dust smeared the legs of her Cruel Girl Jeans and her boots were worn. He could have sworn they were the same boots he'd bought for her birthday a few weeks before they broke up.

Pansy snapped her fingers to get his attention. "Back to you. I want you to tell me the truth about your accident."

That was all she wanted? Hell, he'd tell her about that. No harm in cleaning up the story a little. "Ah, I got throwed off Swamp Fox at the Top Bulls & Cowboys Association bull riding in Nashville. You know, I was having the best year of my life. There wasn't a bull I couldn't ride until I got on that big yellow bastard."

"So you just got thrown off? Why the vacation?" Pansy plucked another clover and twirled the stem between her fingers. She looked up at him, waiting.

Time to reroute these questions. "You know, last year at the finals, he threw me off at seven point nine seconds. The bastard cost me the year-end title. I'd have been the TBC world champion if I could have stayed on for another tenth of a second. This is personal." He looked up to find her watching him the way he used to when they were together.

She always could read him, and he had the sneaking suspicion she knew more than he'd told her.

"How bad were you hurt?"

Kade sat down beside her, his thigh resting against hers. At least this way he didn't have to look her in the eye when he told his white lies. "Not bad. Just thumped my head against the fence. He was a gentleman and didn't step on me."

"A concussion then." She scooted to the edge of the step and leaned against the handrail. "How long were you out?"

There would be no putting Pansy off of this line of questions. "Less than ten minutes. It was nothing really. I feel fine." He leaned back on his elbows and gave her his best smile. It used to work.

"So another grade three concussion. Have you had any others between the one in college and this one?" She raised her hand and touched her fingertips to his forehead. Shaking her head at him, she pulled her hand away. "I can't do this."

She grabbed the handrail and pulled herself to her feet.

As she stood, he rose with her and took her hands in his. "I'm fine. The doctor said I'm good to go in another couple of weeks."

She stared into his eyes, her pupils outlined by the pale blue of her irises.

"Really, my head's fine." He tightened his grip on her fingers, but one by one, they slid from his grip. "Well as good as it's ever been."

She didn't answer, just shook her head, her eyes welling with tears. As always, she knew everything he hadn't said.

~*~

Pansy stood at the kitchen sink. Steam rolled off the hot water as dinner's pans soaked. She'd begged off riding for the last several days. She couldn't face Kade. She couldn't face Willa, and no way was she ready to face her out-of-control feelings.

Her new best friend, Willa, had seemed disappointed Pansy wouldn't ride, but with Kade to help her, she still had fun.

As hard as Pansy had tried to chase hope from her heart, the moment she'd seen him again a tiny dream had hatched—one where Kade gave up riding bulls.

That dream had been blasted into shards of glass, bits that cut her heart to shreds. He might ride for a few more years without another major injury, but she couldn't take the chance.

Pulling a fresh steel wool pad from the box below the sink, she scrubbed at a burned-on speck in the bottom of the last pan. After rinsing it, she placed it in the drainer. As she stood watching the dirty water drain away, she heard voices from the living room.

Cary, Micah and the baby were finally home.

Deep breaths now. This was a happy occasion, she reminded herself. Folding the dishtowel lengthwise, she hung it on the twisted horseshoe Micah used to make a towel rack over the sink. Time to greet the family.

Cary stood, the baby in her arms, just inside the door with a smile as wide as the one on the Cheshire cat. Micah was behind her, his arms full of floral arrangements and presents.

Pansy pulled extra air into her lungs, pasted a smile on her face and went to meet Rodie. She peeked at the tiny, scrunched up face, and her heart gave a little lurch. Little eyes opened, and although she knew babies didn't see very well at this age, she'd swear Rodie looked right at her.

Cary unwrapped him. Tiny crocheted cowboy boots covered his feet, and his onesie had a bucking horse on the front. If this little guy didn't become a cowboy, it wouldn't be his parents' fault.

"Here." Cary handed the baby to Pansy and took off toward the bathroom, one hand cradling her stitches. "I've got to go."

Pansy gazed at the baby, all the time wondering how

she got herself in this mess. Life had been much simpler when she was alone. Having Cary's growing family and Kade and the town of East Hope around provided more commotion in a day than she'd had in all of the last seven years.

Just as she turned toward Micah to hand him his son, she found him watching her.

"Something wrong?"

"Not at all. I'm just glad you're home safe and sound."

"You looked at Rodie like he was a ghost." Micah placed the flowers on the hearth and dropped the baby's bag beside the couch. "What is it?"

She'd opened her mouth, trying to come up with a harmless lie, when they heard a knock. Millie came in carrying a large package. She dropped it to the floor and rushed to take the baby from Pansy.

The older woman peered at Rodie, stroking his cheek with a finger. "You little cutie, you. Who's the best baby boy in the whole wide world? Rodie Owen, that's who." She lifted the baby to her shoulder, a wide smile beaming from her face. "He's adorable, Micah. Where's Cary?"

"She'll be back in a minute." Exhaustion darkened the area beneath Micah's eyes, and Pansy realized just how hard this ordeal had been for him. Against all odds, Cary had found herself a good man.

Maybe . . . No! No use getting her hopes up just to be crushed by reality.

"I'll get us something to drink. Coffee or tea?"

"Either," Millie said, patting the baby on his back.

"I could use a beer." Micah sank onto the couch with a sigh. "Where's my Willa?"

"I saw her in the arena with Kade. I suspect she'll be in as soon as she puts her horse away." Millie walked to the rocker, but before she sat down, she lifted the baby away from her shoulder. "Your big sissy will be in soon, won't she baby? Yes she will."

Before the words were out of her mouth, Willa rushed

through the front door. "Where's my brother? Where's Cary?"

"Doesn't say a lot for me does it?" Micah said as he lifted his daughter and gave her a peck on the cheek. "I missed you Willa Wild."

"Missed you too, Pa, but I gotta see my baby brother." She wiggled until Micah put her down. "He needs me."

"Come on over to the couch, and I'll let you hold him." Millie settled onto the sofa, Willa next to her. She unwrapped the blanket and let Willa get acquainted with her new brother.

The little girl picked up Rodie's hand then touched his toes one by one. She looked from Millie to Micah. "Did he come out of Cary's stomach? 'Cause he looks too big for that."

"Take it, Dad," Millie said. "I'm too old to explain the birds and the bees."

"That's right. Millie explained sex to us, remember?" Kade stood inside the door.

Micah's laugh rang through the room. "Yes, she did, and none to gently if I remember right."

Millie blushed while she settled the baby onto Willa Wild's lap, keeping a hand close.

Kade walked over to the baby. "He looks kind of like you when you were this age, Willa Wild."

"Cept I was prettier, cause I'm a girl."

The next hour sped by, filled with talking, laughing and many, many questions from Micah's daughter.

Pansy stayed in the background, making sure everyone had something to eat, and that Cary didn't try to wait on the others.

There wasn't much to clean after lunch, but she took longer than she could have, before rejoining the group. She watched Cary and Micah with their two children and felt alternating emotions, happiness for her friends, and the sharp, green stab of envy.

"You need to get some rest." Micah helped his wife up

from the couch. "This little guy is going to be up several times tonight."

With lots of hugs and kisses and well wishes, Millie and Clinton took the cue and made their departure.

As Pansy tidied the living room, she looked up to see Kade watching her. In fact, he'd been watching her all day. "What?"

"You're pretty good at distancing yourself from everything and everyone, aren't you?"

It wasn't a question, and she knew it. "I don't know what you mean. I've been right here all along." With a flip of her wrists, Pansy straightened the Pendleton blanket that hung over the back of the couch.

"What do you think of the baby?"

"I think he's a baby. What am I supposed to think?" Her mind had taken to playing a game. On one hand, she wanted nothing more than for Kade to stop prying into her life. On the other hand, if he'd guess at her past and get it right, she could open up.

"You get the same look on your face when you look at Rodie as when you look at Willa. Are you jealous of Cary? You know, of her having kids."

"Nooooo." She'd hope for definitive and got whiny instead. She cleared her throat. "No, Kade, I'm not jealous. I'm just not crazy about kids."

His laughter caught her by surprise, but the look on his face told her he wasn't amused. "You loved kids."

"Loved is the optimum word here. I changed my mind. They're too much trouble." Maybe that would make him back off. She was an evil kid hater, and she knew he loved kids. That's something they'd talked about years before in their *someday conversations*. They'd talked about having kids one day.

One day they did, only Kade wasn't around, and Maxie didn't live.

CHAPTER EIGHT

Whatever thought had just gone through Pansy's mind showed up as pure, red-hot anguish. Kade strode across the room and pulled her into his arms by instinct. He tightened his grip and held her wordlessly.

Her body shuddered and hot tears dampened his shirt.

He wasn't sure how long they stood there, but all too soon, Pansy put her hands on his chest and pushed away.

She ducked her head, refusing to look at him as she picked up the coffee cups scattered on tables around the room.

"Talk to me." Kade followed her into the kitchen. "Please."

When she ignored him, he regrouped. "I want to ask a favor."

Pansy kept her back to him as she washed the dishes. Finally she turned. "I can't promise I'll do it. In fact, I'm pretty sure I won't, but what is it?" She wrung out the dishrag and wiped down the counters as she spoke.

"There's a barrels and bulls event in Bend tonight. I want you to go with me."

"Tonight? No, I can't. I'm helping Cary and Micah. Sorry."

"Micah and Cary will be okay for a few hours. Come on. I promise to leave you alone if you come with me. No more questions." Kade watched as she thought over his proposal. He had no intention stopping his inquiries, but he wasn't about to tell her that.

As Pansy thought about what he'd said, he could read the struggle as it crossed her face.

She didn't want to go anywhere with him, but he'd guessed correctly that she was keeping something from him and wanted the questions to stop.

"This one trip? I go, and then you leave me alone?"

Kade nodded. "No more questions, but I'll listen if you want to talk."

She looked at him from the corner of her eyes, not trusting what he was saying. "I won't want to talk." The reply was flat, not an ounce of ambiguity in any of the five words.

"So you'll come with me?" Kade was afraid to get his hopes up. If he could get her in the truck for the two hours it took to get to Bend maybe they could find a way to reconnect. "We'll leave at four and get dinner on the way. If that's okay with you, that is."

Pansy twisted the chunky turquoise and silver ring she wore on the index finger of her right hand. He'd noticed it the first day he'd seen her again in the café. He'd noticed because she'd never worn jewelry when she was younger. Her father wouldn't have allowed it.

She raised her gaze from the ring. "Okay, but don't worry about dinner. I'm fine."

"No, if I take you on a date, I'm buying dinner." That was the exact wrong thing to say, and Kade knew it the moment the words came out of his mouth. "Not a date. I didn't mean a *date* date, just a mutual trip to an event."

For the first time since the conversation had started, the corners of her lips curved up. It wasn't a smile. It was a not –frown, and that was good enough for him today. Baby steps.

"I'll meet you on the porch at four." Without another word, she hurried upstairs.

By the time Kade fed the animals in the barn, showered and got into his best clothes, he found Pansy sitting on one of the Adirondack chairs, watching the sunset. A picnic basket sat at her feet.

He nodded at the basket. "Packing for an overnight?"

She snorted, and he smiled. When Pansy snorted, it meant she thought whatever was going on was beyond ridiculous and beneath comment. "This is dinner. I packed some leftovers. We can stop along the way."

"I said I'd take you out to dinner."

"Kade, you ride bulls for a living, and you haven't even been able to do that for three months. I'm trying to save you some money, and I don't mind." She stood, picked up the basket and headed for his truck.

It took more than a few minutes to reach Highway Twenty, but he waited until they were headed to Burns before he spoke. "You think I'm broke."

"Do you work another job?" She watched him, her expression kind and filled with pity.

"No, I ride bulls."

"Even if you save a lot, with expenses and all, you can't have much. I've rodeoed, remember. I know how much it pays."

Kade let himself relax. "Have you ever watched a TBC event?"

She shook her head. "I haven't had anything to do with rodeo for a long time."

"It's changed. I've made a good living, better than good. I'd have made quite a bit more if Swamp Fox hadn't thrown me off at the finals last year." He'd never cared much for money, but it felt good to show Pansy he wasn't a loser like she obviously thought. "I've got enough saved to put a good down payment on a ranch when I'm done riding bulls."

Kade focused on the passing landscape as he waited for

her to answer. He'd always liked the high desert. Where others saw dusty desolate hills, he marveled at the pinks and grays, silver-greens and rusts of the sagebrush and the sandstone buttes. He never tired of spotting herds of antelope and mule deer or watching hawks circle above. When he was done competing, this is where he'd call home.

Micah was already keeping an eye out for some ground for him to buy. A nice little ranch for when he was ready to retire.

"And when will you be done?"

Instead of being impressed, she'd asked the one question he wasn't ready to answer.

~*~

Within a few minutes, Kade pulled into the rodeo grounds. The lot behind the arena was filled with horse trailers, cars and pickups. A cattle hauler backed up to a loading chute, opened the gate and a huge speckled bull walked regally down the ramp to the pen, followed by an equally spectacular black one.

"I don't remember them being this big." Pansy leaned against the fence as they watched the rest of the animals unload. The sounds and smells were the same though. She hadn't thought she'd missed this, but rodeo had been a big part of her life for as long back as she could remember. It had been her escape.

If the price hadn't been too high, she'd love it still.

Kade stepped down from where he'd been perched on the fence and took her hand. "Let's go. I want to find Cody."

"Cody?"

"He's a friend of mine. He owns these bulls." He led her through the pens to a gate leading to the arena. They walked down the front of the grandstands toward the bucking chutes.

As the sun settled in the sky, the gloom was chased away by large halogen lights. A tall cowboy with bright red hair climbed over the chute and dropped to the arena floor. He closed the latch on the chute then walked toward them, his grin reminiscent of Howdy Doody. "Hey, Gunslinger."

"Codeman. How ya doin'?" Kade clasped his hand then they did a fancy fist bump. "How many bulls you got here?"

Pansy stepped back, watching the two men interact. By the easy camaraderie and good-natured teasing, she suspected they'd been friends for a long time.

"Pansy, this odd bugger is Cody Matthews. Codeman, this is Pansy Lark."

Pansy stepped forward, warmed by Cody's grin. "Hi, Cody. Nice to meet you." She held out her hand, not sure if she knew how to do the fist bump ritual. She needn't have worried. Cody pulled her into a short hug.

The man stepped back then looked at Kade. "Gunslinger, it doesn't make any difference if we're in New York City or Podunkville, you always find the prettiest ladies, and this one tops the cake."

"Mind your manners, Cody."

The warning fell on deaf ears. Cody turned to Pansy. "Honey, where did this worthless piece of crap find someone like you?"

Kade stepped between Pansy and Cody then threw his arm over her shoulder. "And you never have learned to keep your hands to yourself and your mouth shut."

The touch of jealousy in Kade's voice seemed to make Cody smile. He raised his hands in surrender. "Pansy, when you get tired of the Gunslinger here, you look me up."

"Don't you have something that needs doing?"

Cody's grin widened as he fished in his pocket and pulled out a folded piece of paper. "Day sheet."

As Cody walked away, Kade looked down at the

crumbled paper.

Pansy took it from him and smoothed it on the stadium seats. “Here.”

He folded the day sheet one more time and stuck it in his shirt pocket. Taking Pansy’s hand, he sat then pulled her onto his lap. “Look, he’s just joking. You know, about finding all the women.”

The small jolt of jealousy was gone before she had time to resist it. Kade wasn’t a monk, although the thought of that made her grin.

She’d even had a few flings since she’d left Montana, not that they’d lasted long or meant anything. “You always did have a knack for getting the girls to follow you around.”

“But I didn’t act on it when I was with you.”

The warmth of Kade’s arms around her, and the look in his stormy gray eyes was like a welcome home party. “You never did, but I know you didn’t spend all those years apart pining for me. You had your life, and I had mine.” Not that hers had been so great, but he didn’t need to know that.

He raised his hands and cupped her cheeks. “Pansy, there was never anyone but you.”

When his lips touched hers, a feeling of rightness overwhelmed her. All these years, she’d thought she’d been living. Now she knew she’d merely been surviving.

Pansy gave herself up to the feelings flooding her brain. Loving Kade insured heartache was in her future, but she hadn’t felt so complete since he’d gone.

She ran her fingertips up the back of his neck and tangled them in his hair like she used to, scraping her nails softly over his skin. Kade’s groan set her heart to racing.

When she got back to East Hope, this kind of behavior would have to stop, but for once, she was going to throw caution to the wind and hope the wind didn’t whip it back into her face.

Kade deepened the kiss. His hands roamed up and

down her back as she pressed into him.

She heard a snicker and became aware of more people climbing the stands, searching for the best seat. Pansy put her fingers on Kade's wrists and moved his fingers off her face.

"Let's go somewhere else." His voice was hoarse, his eyes dilated, probably much like her own.

She gave herself a quick lecture on propriety; she was her father's daughter after all. Standing, she pulled away from his warmth. "You brought me to see your friend's bulls. And watching bulls is what we're going to do."

CHAPTER NINE

What the hell was the matter with him? He was acting like a horny teenager, making out with Pansy in the grandstands, but he wasn't sorry one bit. Well, he was sorry she'd shot him down, but she'd always been the sensible one.

She'd pulled his T-shirt from his jeans, and it was a good idea to leave it out. No use getting more ribbing from his friends. He could take it, but Pansy would be embarrassed.

The grandstands had filled almost to capacity. He patted the bench beside him. "Sit down. It's not that long before the show starts."

Pansy reached into her pocket and pulled out a ten-dollar bill. "I'm going to get a couple of beers."

Kade stood. "I'll go with you."

"If you do, we won't have seats when we get back."

Every seat around them was filled, with more people trying to squeeze in. They had a standing room only crowd. Good news for Cody.

He kissed Pansy on the cheek and took his seat. In the past, watching her walk away had always been one of his favorite pass-times. Watching Pansy approach was the only thing better.

He shrugged out of his coat and used it to save her spot. Pulling the day sheet out of his pocket, he ran his finger down the list, finding old friends among both the riders and bulls.

"Kade!"

When he heard his name called, he stood just in time to catch Connie Martin as she threw herself into his arms.

Connie's high-pitched, almost cartoonish voice and boyish figure hid the fact that she was one of the best barrel horse trainers in the country. As far as he knew, a tougher woman had never thrown a leg over a horse.

The brim of Connie's cowboy hat bumped against his then fell to the dirt. Her infectious giggles made him grin. "Where have you been? Don't tell me you retired." She gave him a soft poke in the ribs then bent down for her Resistol.

Kade watched as she finger combed her bangs off her forehead then settled the hat on her head. "Nah, Swamp Fox decided I needed to take a little nap. He used the fence as a sleeping aid."

The smile dropped off Connie's face. "Are you okay?"

"Hey, I'm righter'n rain. I'll be good to enter the finals." Kade moved his coat, and they sat down together. "Good thing I had such a big lead. I'm still hanging in there in the standings."

Connie put her hand on his thigh. "To hell with the standings. How bad was the wreck?"

Kade shook his head. This was Connie. They'd had a thing for a few weeks. The fun had morphed into a solid friendship even though they might go months at a time without seeing each other. "The bastard tried to drive me headfirst through a heavy duty metal panel. Came to about fifteen minutes later. Wasn't sure where or who I was for a couple of days. My head still hurts like a bitch when I over do, but…"

He looked up to see Pansy standing about five feet

away, a beer in each hand. Had she heard what he'd told Connie? "I'm feeling great now. All healed up. Doc says I'm ready to go."

Connie drew her brows together, obviously confused by the quick change of direction.

Kade jumped to his feet, took one of the beers from Pansy and handed it to Connie. Pansy's fingers were icy cold, and he wrapped his hand around hers. "Pansy, this is my good friend, Connie Martin. Connie, meet my old friend, Pansy Lark."

Pansy took a long pull on her beer, pulled her hand free and held it out to Connie. "Nice to meet you. I'm always glad to meet Kade's *good* friends."

Connie looked at Kade, obviously trying to figure out who the woman was. There wasn't enough time in the world to explain that. Not knowing what to say, he shrugged.

Connie took Pansy's hand. "I met Kade back east quite a few years ago."

It was Pansy's turn to shrug. "He seems to get around."

Connie's smile was puzzled as she handed the beer back to Kade. "Hey, good to meet you, but I've got to get Frenchie ready to run. I'm up in the first draw. See you later, Kade." Before he could answer, she'd disappeared into the crowd.

Pansy took another swallow then studied the beer label like it held the secret to curing cancer. "So she's a good friend and I'm old?"

Aw, hell! That had been as awkward as a donkey in dance class. "I didn't handle that very well. Connie is a good friend. That's all, a friend."

"You don't have to explain. In fact, I can find another ride home if I'm in the way."

Kade pulled her down beside him and wrapped his arm around her. She would have no trouble at all finding a ride or anything else she wanted around this bunch of guys. "No."

She looked at him, her eyebrows raised at the abrupt tone of his voice.

He should explain, make her feel better, but the only word he could utter was *No.*

The National Anthem saved him from having to come up with coherent conversation. By the time they sat down again, the first six bulls were loaded in the chutes, and the cowboys were pulling their ropes.

"Ladies and Gentlemen, tonight is the inaugural performance of the annual Bend, Oregon Bulls and Barrels. We've got the rankest bulls, the stickiest cowboys and the fastest, prettiest cowgirls this side of Timbuktu."

Excitement filled the arena as people shifted in their seats. A murmur traveled through the crowd. The stands were filled with rodeo connoisseurs, ready for the thrills of the bulls.

"I don't know the first rider, but the bull should put on a great show. I rode him to win Tulsa last year." These were Kade's kind of people and as much as he'd liked spending time in East Hope, there was nothing like being entered. Anticipation got his blood pumping.

"First out is Bobby Thompson on Lazy Daze. Folks, this bull was bucking bull of the year in the Top Bulls and Cowboys Association two years ago." The announcer continued to wade through statistics about the bulls and cowboys, but Kade's attention was on the chute gate.

As the gate swung open, the big, black baldy bull stood on his hind legs and leaped into the arena. He slung his head to the right then spun to the left. The cowboy made it one full wrap before being tossed to the side like a discarded toy.

Kade heard Pansy's intake of breath.

"Isn't that cat cool?" If they'd let him get on right now, he'd be in the arena in two seconds. One of his favorite rides had been aboard Lazy Daze. When Pansy didn't answer, he looked up to see her watching him. He picked up her hand and laced his fingers through hers. "You used to like bull riding."

The disillusionment in her slight smile hit him like a slap across the face. "I used to like a lot of things, and then I grew up."

~*~

Kade was lit from the inside like he'd swallowed a halogen lamp. Leaning forward with his hands clasped, he bounced his forearms repeatedly on his thighs. Electric energy had wafted off him in waves. During the few seconds the black bull bucked, he'd almost levitated into the arena to help the kid ride.

Pansy made an effort to relax the tension in her jaw. What had she expected? This was Kade's whole life. If he couldn't ride bulls, he couldn't breathe.

At her words, his excitement faded. "You really don't want to watch this? We can leave."

Great! Now he was being nice. "No, I'd like to stay. Your friend is up in the barrels soon." The friend who was so thin she'd almost blow away.

All through high school and college, Pansy had dieted trying to get that kind of figure. She'd come close, but it took an iron will and a manic passion for vegetables.

Pansy'd stopped dieting when she lost the baby. She had no one to please but herself, and she didn't care about a few pounds anymore. She liked the way she looked. Besides, it would be hard to fill out the Marilyn costume if she was flat chested.

All her mental work didn't prevent a flash of envy from racing through her heart before she stuffed that crap back where it had come from. So what if Connie was a size two. So what if Kade had said she trained and competed on great barrel horses. So what if she'd been Kade's number-one BFF for all these years.

Okay, that was one *So what* too many.

"I can't wait to see Connie run. Does she have a really

nice horse?" A little white lie never hurt anyone, right? Pansy turned her attention to the arena, hoping Kade bought the story.

Kade touched her shoulder.

She turned back and gave him her best smile.

With a gaze filled with questions, he shrugged. "He's just a six year old. They cleaned up at the futurities last year, and she's been winning pretty steady. His name is Frenchman's Renown."

She shrugged.

Kade kept his attention on the arena while the grounds crew set up the barrels. "He's a grandson of Frenchman's Guy, the all-time leading barrel horse sire, and has been making a name for himself in the barrel racing circles."

Seems like everyone associated with rodeo assumed everyone else kept track of horses. She shook her head. "I remember Frenchman's Guy, kind of."

He explained the famous horses she might know that were from this lineage.

Pansy took the opportunity to revel in his familiar looks. He was the most handsome man she'd ever known, both then and now. Just the sight of him had warmed her girl parts and still did.

Kade's skin was the same dark tan from all the hours he spent in the sun. High cheekbones and an aquiline nose gave him a classic profile, more suited to a suit than Wranglers and boots. But he was all cowboy, always had been.

"We're ready to begin our first section of barrel racers, and first out is Connie Martin on her great young horse Frenchman's Renown."

As Connie's horse burst through the gate the crowd jumped to their feet. Pansy joined them.

The sleek palomino gelding ran full speed, driving around the barrel so close Pansy sucked in a breath. He didn't lose any speed for the rest of the run.

Having qualified for the college rodeo national finals

three times, Pansy remembered the rush of racing at the barrels on a great horse. She'd been pretty good, had loved it at the time, but Connie was so much more than that.

Connie was an extension of her horse. As the pair ran out of the arena, the crowd roared.

Pansy missed the camaraderie, the competition and the completeness rodeo had given her. But she'd never go back. It was an expensive sport to be sure, but the emotional cost was what she couldn't afford.

The rest of the event went by as a blur for Pansy. Barrel racers and bull riders all did their best, but she spent most of the time watching Kade. It was obvious this was where he longed to be, and the one thing Pansy knew for sure, she wasn't waiting another seven years for him to be ready to settle down. She sighed with relief when the last bull rider rode the last bull.

As they walked away from the arena, they heard someone call to Kade.

"Where are you two going?" Cody hurried over to them. "We're all meeting up at Brother Jon's for a couple of beers."

Pansy's heart clenched. The last thing she wanted to do was sit with a bunch of rodeo cowboys and cowgirls. Connie would probably be there, and if not her, there would be other women hitting on Kade. They always had, but she'd never been jealous before. She'd trusted him, and he'd never let her down. He'd never even paid attention to the buckle bunnies other than to be polite.

It was not that she was jealous now. Okay, she was a little jealous, but she had no right. They were over, and soon he'd be gone.

Kade gave her hand a little squeeze before answering Cody. "Not tonight. We've got to get home."

Had he realized she'd be uncomfortable, or maybe he just didn't want to hang out with these people tonight? She'd go with the last one. No way did she want to think about him being able to read her thoughts like he used to.

"Then before you go, I wanted to ask you something." Words spilled over each other in Cody's haste to get them out. He'd obviously been thinking about this subject for a while. "I'd like to partner up with you. You know, with the bulls. I need some help, and I can't think of anyone I'd rather work with."

She felt Kade stiffen, but the smile on his face didn't waver. "You're just feeling sorry for me because I got hurt. I heard you were doing great on your own."

"That's not true. I've got some great bulls, and I'm making a good living, but there's room for someone else."

Kade shook his head the whole time Cody spoke, his mind apparently made up.

For a split second at Cody's first words, Pansy felt hope rise in her chest. It didn't take long for that emotion to die a quick death. She knew in her heart Kade wouldn't quit entering a moment before age or injury made it impossible for him to pull his bull rope.

"Man, I'm a bull rider, not a business man," Kade said. "I won't be around here much—for the next few years anyway."

He not only wasn't a businessman, he wasn't husband or daddy material.

Cody nodded. "You think about it. You've got lots of contacts, and you know bulls. We could do good together." With a wave, he turned and headed toward the pens housing the bulls.

"Too bad it isn't a few years down the road." Kade took her hand as they headed toward where he'd parked the truck. "Might be fun."

They walked across the dark, dusty parking lot in silence. Kade laced his fingers through hers, stroking his thumb across her palm. His touch sent a cascade of sparks shooting along her nerve endings. The desire to give in and enjoy him for whatever time she had left was almost overwhelming, but his words kept ringing through her head. "I won't be around here much—for the next few years anyway."

CHAPTER TEN

When Kade pulled up to the ranch house, the only light visible was a faint stream filtering through the kitchen window curtains. Even Micah and Cary's bedroom window was dark. Little Rodie, along with his parents and sister, must be asleep.

Kade hurried around the front of the Dodge and caught up with Pansy before she got to the porch steps. "Come to the barn with me. We need to talk."

When they'd first arrived in Bend, Pansy'd seemed to be enjoying herself. She'd commented on the scenery during the drive in, talked about the café and shared the sandwiches she'd made for the trip. She'd even seemed a little excited to watch the bulls.

It had been almost like old times, but sometime during the bull riding, or maybe it was the barrel race, she'd become quiet.

If Kade asked a question, she answered readily enough, but her smile had disappeared like smoke on a windy day.

The two-hour drive home had been made in near silence.

"We said everything important years ago. I'm tired." She turned to face him, and the look on her face stopped his heart. Sadness rolled off her in waves. "Thank you for a nice evening."

"This is important." Kade laid his hand on her forearm then nodded to the dark hulking shadow of the barn and waited. He needed to clear the air. "Please."

Pansy shrugged. She shook off his hand and strode toward the barn, her spine stiff, her body tense.

Kade tugged on the wooden handle and swung open the smaller door on the west side. He stood back and let Pansy enter first then followed her to the bench beside the tack room.

She sat down, but when he sat beside her, she stood and crossed to the other side of the aisle. "What's so important that it couldn't wait until morning?"

The bare yellow bulb overhead swung slightly on its cord, throwing faint, eerie shadows across the two by eight walls. Pale moonlight slipped through the small, high window and brightened a square on the floor.

Kade stretched out a leg and dipped the toe of his boot into the spot of light.

How was he supposed to start? If he didn't get this right, he had a feeling Pansy wouldn't give him another chance. He'd never been accused of being faint of heart, so he sucked in a breath and blurted out what was on his mind. "What's important *is* us. What are we going to do about us?"

In the back of Kade's mind, he'd been mulling over how to bring this up to Pansy. Everything had felt right since he'd found her again, and he wanted to make things great once more. He'd be done riding bulls in a few years, and making a life with this woman was at the top of his list.

The question hadn't come out the way he'd planned. He'd been going for a little more romance, but at least he'd started something.

He'd been staring at the toes of his boots and finally risked looking at her.

Anger, pure and hot, colored her face. She stormed down the center aisle of the barn, the heels of her boots sending up puffs of dust. When she reached the end, she turned and came back at him like a bullet. "There is no us!" Her voice wavered, her hands closed into fists and her eyes shot sparks. "There hasn't been an us since you abandoned me."

"Abandoned you?" He'd known she still harbored resentment for the way things ended, but abandoned? "I never hid the fact that riding bulls was what I wanted to do with my life. You knew that."

"You went and had fun while I cleaned up the mess you left behind."

"What mess? I know your parents weren't the best, but you graduated college, and you've done just fine without me." It rankled him that she'd done better than okay without him. "What mess?"

The anger and rage drained out of her like air from a punctured balloon. She dropped to the floor, leaning her head back onto the stall wall. "I was pregnant." Her voice shook as she said the words.

"Wait." Kade was having a hard time following the quick change of subjects. "You said you lost a baby. You said it wasn't mine. Was it?"

Pansy nodded without raising her head.

"You lost my baby?" Kade could hardly get the words out.

Pansy's head snapped up. "It's not like I did it on purpose." She scrambled to her feet, but then seemed at a loss at what to do next.

Kade stood and caught hold of her hand. "I didn't mean that like it sounded. Start at the beginning. Tell me what happened."

Pansy sucked in a shaky breath then let it out with a whoosh. She worked her hand free from his and folded them together, her fingers clenched tight over her knuckles. "Look, it's over and there's nothing we can do to fix things."

"If I'm the baby's father, I deserve to know what happened."

Her breath came in short, shallow pants. Bright pink flushed across her cheeks. She lifted her hands and slammed them into his chest. "You…" The strident sound of her voice seemed to bring her back from her fury. Backing away, she stared at him, her jaw clenched. "I tried to call you—several times."

"After you—"

Pansy held up a hand palm out. "When I called you the last time after you left, I know I fell apart. I didn't know I was pregnant when I made that call, although that helps explain why I lost it." She stuffed her hands into the back pockets of her jeans, pacing in a circle around him.

They'd barely had a fight the whole time they'd dated, so he'd been baffled by her phone call. She'd cried, screamed and begged. She'd even resorted to threats. "You scared me. You were out of control. You weren't the girl I'd known." Looking back, he should have seen something was very wrong with Pansy, but back then it had been easier to ignore the drama.

"Just listen."

No matter how hard it was for him to keep quiet, he owed it to Pansy to hear her out. He wondered if she'd ever told anyone what had happened after he left.

"I called you several more times and left messages. You never answered my calls. When I realized you weren't coming back, I went to my parents." The humorless chuckle she released was filled with all kinds of sad.

Kade knew what kind of support those people would give to their only daughter. Not one bit if it didn't go along with their religious views.

"Dad told me to get rid of it." Tears filled her eyes. She blinked trying to hold them back, but one broke free and rolled a silvery trail down her cheek. "He called my baby an it. Like she didn't mean anything at all."

Kade slid his hands beneath his thighs. If he didn't, he'd gather her into his arms. And he was pretty sure she wouldn't stand for that. "That's when you left?"

She nodded.

"You could have gone to Mom and Dad. They love you like you're their own daughter."

"Papa made it clear I wasn't to tell anyone in town. He didn't want the embarrassment of his child being an unwed mother." Pansy reached down and plucked up a piece of straw. Keeping her gaze on the pale yellow stalk, she continued. "And you didn't return my calls. Why would I go to your parents?"

Kade's parents would have been overjoyed at the thought of any grandchild, but especially Pansy's child. They'd loved her for almost as long as he had. "You didn't think they would want to know?"

~*~

"Hard as this is for you to believe, I wasn't really thinking about you or your family. I was trying to find a place to live and food to eat." Pansy's tone was sharp, filled with the pain of years past as she told another white lie. She'd thought of Kade every moment of every day for years.

She raised her gaze and stared into his eyes. "Do you know how hard it is to be all alone? To have no one and to be scared to death?"

He watched her, his eyes searching for her deepest private thoughts. "Tell me about the baby."

Pain flooded her system. A moan escaped as she wrapped her arms around her waist, but when Kade reached for her, she pushed him away. If she gave in to his kindness now, she'd never get through this without breaking down.

Now that he knew the baby was his, Kade wouldn't give up until he knew every detail. She rocked back and forth, trying to put her words in order, trying to tell him about his daughter. "I was just over six months along when I doubled over at work. A friend took me to the free clinic. It was too late."

Kade turned away and walked to the end of the building. He stood with his back to her.

As Pansy waited, she looked around the barn. Years ago, when she'd still held out hope Kade would find her, she'd imagined this scenario. She'd imagined Kade finding her in Denver. She'd never thought the difficult conversation would take place in a dusty barn.

Although Denver had provided the anonymity she'd sought, it was big, and she was a country girl at heart. Several times she'd thought of leaving, but she didn't have the heart to start over. Besides, Maxie's tiny grave was there.

She'd walked like a zombie through her days, not really living. Not until she'd met Cary and come here had things looked up.

Kade turned and strode back to her. "Did we—" He stopped and cleared his throat. "Did we have a daughter or a son?"

She'd lived with their baby's death for years and had come to terms with it as much as possible, but watching Kade, she realized the knife sharp pain of loss was just starting for him.

"I named our daughter Maxie. You'd have liked her, Kade. She was a fighter.

"She lived for a while?"

"Eight days, but in the end, she was just too little." She'd had that all-too-short time with their daughter, something Kade would never get. "I told her how much I loved her. I told her about you." Her voice cracked and tears filled her eyes.

"You named her Maxie?" Kade had stopped pacing and turned his full attention to her.

"Maxine Eleanor Lucie. I named her for my

grandmother, your mom and Eleanor Roosevelt. I figured it couldn't hurt to have people as strong as those three women to watch over her." Even though logically she knew it wasn't true, she'd often wondered if Grams and Mrs. Roosevelt thought she couldn't take care of Maxie and had called her to be with them.

"My mom will be honored. Would you come with me to tell them?" Kade stood in front of her, his arms hanging at his sides. "They'll want to know."

The thought of standing in front of Kade's parents, the people who'd made her life bearable, and telling them their granddaughter had died made her lungs seize. She coughed, trying to clear her throat. "I don't know if I can do that."

"Do you want to keep this just between us?" Kade reached out, touching her arm with his fingertips.

She stopped, took a deep breath and took his hand in hers. "I know this is all new to you, but I've finally made peace with Maxie's death. I not sure I can go through this all again. Not now. I'm not that girl who did everything everybody asked no matter how hard it was on her."

Kade's confusion and pain were evident in his expression. "I didn't mean to hurt you, Pansy. If I'd known—"

The sight of his eyes filling with tears did her in. She turned away and sank to her knees. The anger she'd harbored for Kade melted away like a late spring snowstorm. He hadn't known. They'd both been kids. He'd done the best he could with what he knew, and she'd somehow muddled through and came out the other side whole—but not undamaged.

Kade dropped down beside her and gathered her into his arms. "Maxie. I like that." He rocked her slowly, rubbing her back and humming nonsense in her ear.

When she'd regained some control, she leaned back, placing her palm against the stubble on his cheek. She'd missed this closeness, the absolute knowledge this was where she belonged, the love she felt in her bones and her heart.

Pansy leaned forward and pressed her forehead to his. She tried to talk, to sound like an adult, but her voice came out a whisper. "Maxie would have loved you."

Kade pulled her onto his lap and wrapped his arms around her, encasing her in his warmth. "What can I do to make this better?" He kissed her softly on the lips, sending a tidal wave of shivers down her spine.

The words came unbidden to her mind. She barely kept from blurting them out.

Don't ride another bull!

It was the one thing she wanted from him, and the one thing she couldn't ask. When the day came that Kade quit being a bull rider, he'd have to make that decision for himself.

She knew she could force it. With all the guilt he was feeling right now, Pansy didn't have a doubt he'd do anything she asked. And he'd come to regret it.

Her smile was as close to happy as she could make it. She hoped he wouldn't notice the tension wavering in the corners of her mouth. "There's nothing we can do about the past. We're different people now. Let's just go on from here and see how things work out."

Kade drew her into a kiss as deep and hot as a geothermal pool, melting her reservations and the ice that had encased her heart since Maxie had died. When he drew back, he whispered, "I've always loved you."

Could it be that everything she'd ever wanted was within her grasp?

Years of hard knocks had taught her to be careful, to look the gift horse right in the mouth and count its teeth.

She disentangled herself and rose from his lap. "I loved you, and I still do, but I can't risk you leaving again."

Kade stood beside her. He took a strand of her hair between his fingers and gave it a soft tug. "Who says I'm going to leave?"

Pansy couldn't contain the snort of derision, or maybe that was the sound of reality giving her the boot again. "You've already entered the finals, haven't you?"

God, how she wanted him to deny her words.

Kade shook his head. "Of course I've entered. I've still got an outside chance to win the World Championship, and if I draw Swamp Fox, I'll prove to everyone I can ride the toughest bull around. You can come with me."

She could tell by the look on Kade's face he thought he'd come up with the answer to their problems. He thought he could have her and ride bulls.

Pansy's heartbeat sped up. He still didn't get it. "When you left, it broke my heart. And when I lost Maxie, it broke me, all of me. But in the back of my mind, I knew that even if I never saw you again, you were somewhere, alive and well. If you're killed, I don't think I could ever recover."

Kade laughed. "You think a bull's going to kill me? Believe me, that is not going to happen. I'm a professional."

"Being a professional didn't keep that bull at the college rodeo or Swamp Fox from knocking you out." The sight of Kade unconscious in the arena at the long ago rodeo flashed into her mind. She was glad she hadn't been there at the TBC event. "Bull riding is a dangerous sport, and you've been lucky. I can't be there when your luck runs out."

CHAPTER ELEVEN

Kade poured water into the fancy coffee maker Cary had installed in the kitchen shortly after she moved in and started it brewing. He was the first one up this morning, and he wanted to get out of the house before he saw Pansy.

He'd told her he was going to help Cody put on a bull-riding school for the local high school boys. And he was. He hadn't lied. He just hadn't mentioned he might get on a practice bull or two.

When he came home unharmed, she would see he was right. Except for that bump on the head, he was invincible.

Omission is a lie. The singsong voice of his damn conscience kept shouting its unsolicited opinion.

But women were complex creatures. At least, that's what his buddies had told him over and over. He'd have to take their word for it. The young Pansy hadn't been complicated, and since they'd been apart, he'd never stayed with one woman long enough to see for himself.

He wasn't asking that much. Just for the woman he loved to have faith in him and trust him. He didn't give much credence to her crazy fears. Anyone with eyes in their heads could see he was at the top of his game.

And he wasn't leaving Pansy behind again. He'd have to reassure her of that. Instead of traveling with the guys, she could go to every event with him. Waking up to her pretty face was much better than the scruffy mugs of his friends.

He wasn't going to get killed on a bull. He'd been riding for years and only been hurt once. Well, maybe twice if you counted that time in college. Not bad considering most bull riders have more than their fair share of broken bones and torn muscles.

Convincing Pansy that he'd be fine would take some work, but she'd come around. At this point, leaving her again wasn't an option.

After giving him a quick, hard kiss good night, Pansy'd hurried to the house, leaving him alone with his thoughts and plans. Another couple of hours flew by before he hit the sack. He'd only gotten a few hours sleep, but he could feel energy crawling along his nerve endings. The sharp shot of adrenalin he felt at the thought of straddling a bull gave him all the boost he needed.

He wasn't the kid who thought he had to prove himself. He was a man with a goal in mind and a woman he loved.

He poured a thermos of coffee and drove across town to the rodeo arena. Cody was already there along with a group of excited teen-aged cowboys. "Gunslinger, you ready to rock?"

Cody walked from the bucking chutes toward three bulls standing in the middle of the pen. He tapped the big red one with a sorting stick. and with a low bellow, the huge animal moved into the alleyway leading to the chutes.

A trill of excitement raced through Kade's veins. He'd missed riding like he'd miss breathing. "Let's get these kids molded into bull riders."

A cheer went up from the boys then a groan when Cody told them they'd have some learning to do before they'd be allowed to climb on a bull's back.

"You guys are wasting my time." The gangly kid stood out from the others. His expensive new chaps and shiny spurs hadn't ever been on a bull. From the looks of it, they hadn't been on the kid for long. "I came here to ride bulls."

"We do safety first." Cody frowned at the young man. "You don't like that, you can leave."

Kade walked over and held out his hand. "Kade Vaughn."

The kid looked at the others, a grin spreading across his angular face. "Tuff Hanson. One of these days I'm going to ride better than you." He shook Kade's hand, squeezing until the muscles in his arm jumped.

Kade squeezed back, barely containing his smile as Tuff twisted his hand, finally managing to pull his fingers free. "Well, Tuff. You'll have to put your spurs on the right feet if you want to make eight seconds on anything more than a stick horse."

Bravado left the young cowboy like air from a popped balloon. As the others laughed, he sat on the ground and switched his spurs.

Kade had to give him credit. Once he stopped trying to be the toughest man there, he shut up and listened.

The hours sped by, hurried along by the kids excitement, laughter and nerves. By the end of the day, each boy had gotten on at least two bulls and one of them had even ridden the full eight seconds.

It was nearly dark when they got the young men headed home. They had just enough daylight for Kade to get his chance to ride.

Tuff still stood by the arena sulking because his parents were late.

"Hey kid. Get over here and make yourself useful." Cody ran in a black and white spotted bull he called Big Bopper.

Tuff dropped his riggin bag and ran to the bucking chutes. "What do you need me to do?" He turned to Kade.

"Want me to pull your rope?"

"Open the gate, but not until I nod."

Tuff scrambled to the front of the chute, his hand on the latch before Kade settled on the bull. He was focused on Kade.

Bopper turned his head, looking through the gate at Tuff. He was an unusually big animal, gentle as a kitten and not particularly a hard bull to ride. Perfect for Kade's first out.

Years of practice took over as Kade settled onto the broad back. Bopper stood like a statue while Cody helped him pull his bull rope. When Kade nodded his head, Tuff slid the latch and swung the gate open.

Just like a remote control toy, Bopper made his classic moves, leaping out of the chute then spinning to the right. Kade would have ridden for an hour if it wouldn't have tired the bull. He stepped off the animal, ran to the fence and did a fist pump for the sheer joy of riding again. "Woohoo!"

"Gunslinger is back!" Cody opened the exit gate, and Bopper walked out of the arena with all the decorum of a Supreme Court Justice. With a shake of his mismatched horns, he stopped to rub his head on the gatepost before ambling out the gate to the hay he knew was waiting.

"I was born to do this." Kade picked up his bull rope and walked to the chute. "Got another one?"

Cody laughed. "I have twenty more if you want 'em."

"One more will do today." Kade gathered his bull rope from off the arena floor and climbed the bucking chute. The feeling of rightness at being where he belonged, brought a big smile to his face. "I'll ride the other nineteen tomorrow."

The second bull, High Times, was a lot tougher to ride than Bopper. He turned back both ways and spun like a tornado for the last four seconds. Kade handled him with ease. He hadn't lost a move during his recovery.

When they had the bulls settled in the pens, he helped

Cody feed. On the drive back to Micah's, he was almost as excited as the high school kids had been about having another day to ride.

Kade rolled down the windows, turned off the radio and rehearsed what he was going to say to Pansy. She'd understand. She had to.

Bright lights glowed from the downstairs windows when he pulled up to the farmhouse. Someone was still up. Hopefully, it was Pansy.

Kade bounded up the steps and finding the living room empty, he hurried to the kitchen.

Micah sat in a chair, Rodie on his shoulder. He jiggled the baby as he grinned at Kade. "You look like you won the lottery."

"Sit down." Cary gave him a grin. "I'll get you some pie."

"Did you have a good time teaching baby bull riders?" Micah had ridden bulls in high school, but as he got older, he'd decided his place was on the ranch.

"A couple of them have some talent. The Barker boy is the best." Kade forked a bite of cherry pie into his mouth, groaning with pleasure as the sweetness of the fruit exploded over his taste buds. "You are a magician, Cary. This stuff is lethal."

Cary took the baby from Micah. "This little cowboy needs to go to bed. I'll see you later." As she started out of the kitchen, Kade stopped her.

"Where's Pansy? I want to tell her about today."

Cary froze then turned to look at her husband. "We thought she was with you."

"She was gone when we got up." Micah stood and hurried up the stairs with Kade on his heels.

Pansy's room was hauntingly neat, all of her belongings gone.

Micah turned to Kade. "Maybe she went back to town."

"Maybe." But Kade doubted it. If she'd just gone

home, she'd have told the Wests or at the very least, written a note. "I'm going to go check."

The drive out to the ranch had been filled with hope. The drive to Pansy's apartment was filled with dread. He couldn't think of a realistic scenario that ended with him being happy. If she hadn't left town, she'd have dropped by to watch the school, not crept out without telling anyone.

A security light cast a weak yellow glow on the stairs leading to the apartment above the café. He hurried up and rapped on the door. It swung open at his touch. A clean plate sat on the counter, an empty glass in the sink.

"Pansy?" He called to her, but he knew she was gone. The vibrancy that surrounded her had disappeared. "Damn it, Pansy!"

Shivering, Kade walked out the door and sank to the rough wooden step. Losing Pansy hurt like a bitch. He stared into nothing as traffic sounds faded and lights blinked out one by one in the neighboring houses and apartments.

The open door to the apartment taunted him. Pansy was gone.

He hurried down the steps to his truck. Was this payback? Was she that vindictive? Well, if she couldn't support him, couldn't see how much this meant to him, fuck it!

~*~

For five days, seven hours and twelve minutes, Pansy had worked hard to not think about Kade. And for almost that long, she'd failed miserably.

At least twice a day and sometimes three times, she'd made up her mind to quit Romeo's again and make her way back to East Hope. Each time she'd stopped herself. If Kade wouldn't at least listen to her point of view, they'd never make it.

Luigi had been ecstatic when she'd applied for the sous chef position. He'd even refrained from cussing her out for a day or two.

Not one of the other servers and line chefs had been here when she'd left. With Luigi's temper tantrums, no one stayed long. New people didn't bother her though. She kept her distance and stayed to herself.

"I need table seven's order now," bellowed the over weight, ill-mannered executive chef. He slammed a pan down on the counter as if he thought they couldn't hear his screeching growl. "Or heads are going to roll."

"We're working on it." Pansy turned to the quaking grill chef, Marta, and smiled at the woman. "What can I do to help?"

"Run over Luigi with your car?" Marta managed a shaky smile. "Make that a truck."

"Oh, honey. I'd like to. It's one of my fantasies." Pansy laid her hand on Marta's shoulder. "But I don't have a truck."

Pansy saw Marta stiffen as the young woman's eyes widened. Her gaze was fixed on something over Pansy's left shoulder.

"You can borrow mine." The deep, whiskey rich voice seeped through her skin and into her bones.

She'd read that a person's imagination could do strange things. Hers had been trying to conjure up Kade since she'd left East Hope. Looked like it had succeeded.

When she turned, he stood inside the back door to the kitchen looking even more delectable than he had the last time she'd seen him.

Why the hell was he was here?

Didn't he know what he did to her?

Go away, she wanted to shout at him. She wanted to ask all the questions, but her throat was on strike, and the words were locked up. All she could do was stare, fill her memory for when he was gone again.

"Can we go somewhere and talk?" Kade stepped

closer, crowding her against the polished metal prep counter.

"I'm working." She tried to move around him, but he put his arms on either side, holding her in place.

"Okay, we'll do this here, in front of an audience." He leaned in and gave her a quick kiss before she could turn away.

Pansy heard a cake tin drop to the floor, the clattery sound ringing through the now silent kitchen. The entire staff had come to a standstill, including Luigi. All eyes were trained on the two of them.

Kade put a fingertip on her chin and tipped her face so she had to look at him. "I love you."

She swore she heard several of the women sigh. Great, the man had been here less than five minutes, and he already had the women employees on his side, probably a couple of the men, too.

Determined not to get into a verbal tug of war with him, she remained silent.

"I love you more than anything, including riding bulls." The voice was Kade's, and the words were ones she'd longed to hear for years.

If only she could believe him.

"I'm drawing out of the finals. I've talked to Cody and Micah. I'm going into business with Cody." The smile that scrambled her brain spread across his full mouth. "Get this. I'm Cody's marketing director among other things. Those business classes from college will come in handy after all."

She raised her brows. And waited for the other shoe to fall.

"Micah found a couple of ranches in East Hope. We can look at them when we get back, or we can move to Montana, closer to my folks." Kade leaned closer, so close she could feel his breath on her neck. "I love you. Tell me what you want."

He was willing to give up everything he'd worked for,

everything he loved to make her happy.

She'd yearned for this, but now that she had it, she couldn't take advantage.

Even if he never had one regret about retiring, she would always know. She'd know she'd kept him from his dreams. She'd be the one who kept Kade Vaughn from becoming a world champion.

"I want you safe." Her voice was a whisper.

"Okay," Kade said. "I'll do my best." His lips brushed hers in a soft promise.

"And I want you to ride the hair off of Swamp Fox and all the other bulls you draw at the finals."

He was nodding, agreeing to anything, but when he realized what she'd said, he froze.

She almost laughed at his confusion. Leaning forward, she kissed him until her head swam. Pulling back, she touched his lips with her fingertips. If she didn't say what was on her mind now, she was afraid she'd never get it out. "I want you to win, not for the money, not for the recognition, but for you."

Wrapping his hands around waist, Kade boosted her onto the counter. "I think I can do that. What changed your mind?"

"You. If you and bull riding are a package, I guess I have to take both. Will you do one thing for me?" She wrapped her arms around his neck and pulled him close. Putting her lips to his ear, she whispered, "Wear a helmet."

Kade lifted her up and spun in a circle. When he stood her on her feet, he grinned. "I won't kid you. I don't like the idea of wearing a helmet. It just doesn't feel western, but if that's what you want, sweetheart, you got it."

~*~

The flashing lights and compelling sounds of the slot machines kept Pansy's attention partially diverted during most of their week in Las Vegas. She even kind of had fun, right up until the minute Kade left her to get ready to ride.

Micah and Cary had brought the kids, and Clinton surprised Millie with the trip. Even Cheney and Henry had flown in with Wanda Lu.

The senior citizens of East Hope were doing Vegas, and Pansy hoped Vegas was prepared.

Her whole adopted family was here to support Kade. Their excited chatter surrounded her, but no matter how she tried, Pansy couldn't concentrate on her friends. Excusing herself, she found an empty seat at the top of the arena bleachers.

She'd spent each of the last six nights in the hotel, counting the minutes, waiting for word of Kade's safety. Tonight, for the final ride of the season, he'd asked her to come watch.

His finals had been picture perfect, and Kade was only a few points out of first place in the standings. It would all come down to this last ride.

When Pansy'd heard he'd drawn Swamp Fox in the last round, she longed to ask him to draw out, but with a million dollars to the winner, Kade was pumped.

The money wouldn't mean a thing if he was injured.

During the introductions, Kade stood in the arena, his helmet in his hand. He'd complained each night, but true to his word, he'd worn the helmet for each ride.

The announcer went into his rehearsed speech as Kade crawled into the chute and lowered himself onto his bull. Cody kept a grip on the back of his vest in case the bull threw a fit in the chute. But Swamp Fox stood quietly, a professional waiting his chance to perform.

Pansy covered her face with her hands when she saw Kade nod, but couldn't resist peeking through her fingers.

Exploding from the chute as if shot from a cannon, the bull soared so high Pansy wasn't sure if he'd come down at all. How could a one-ton animal be so athletic? Awesome didn't come close to describing Swamp Fox.

The bull hit the ground, immediately leaping into the

air again, his big, yellow body twisting until his belly pointed at the ceiling.

If the massive animal fell and crushed Kade, she'd never forgive herself, but the bull landed on his feet with ease. Slinging his head to the left, his spin gained speed until he and Kade were almost a blur.

Just when she thought Kade had bested the bull, Swamp Fox reversed direction so fast Kade tipped to the outside of the spin. The roar from the crowd filled the arena. Throwing his left arm across his body, Kade adjusted to the bull's move at the last second.

Her cowboy rode with the grace of a dancer, and Pansy realized for the first time, just how good he was.

Black dots floated before her eyes. She was going to pass out if she didn't breathe. She sucked in a breath just as she heard the signal ending the eight seconds.

Before the sound of the buzzer had even faded away, Kade flew off the bull's back, arms flailing, before landing hard. She could almost hear him hit the ground.

Swamp Fox continued bucking over top of Kade, the bull's hind feet coming dangerously close to his head with each spin.

Pansy knew the clowns here were the best in the business. They worked expertly as a team, but as they moved the bull away from him, she buried her face in her hands. Tears burned her eyes, and she was having trouble getting enough air into her lungs. This was her worst nightmare come to life.

People on either side of her rose to their feet, and the crowd erupted in cheers. The sound rocketed from side to side of the arena.

With her heart pounding, Pansy stood and peered over the shoulder of the woman in front of her. As she watched, Cody ran to Kade and stuck out his hand.

Kade clasped it, staggering to his feet. Searching the arena seats, he found the spot where his friends from East Hope were sitting and waved. As Cody pounded him on the back, he did a silly, awkward dance.

A soft giggle escaped from Pansy's tight lungs as tears rolled down her face. For a man with the agility of a cat, Kade couldn't dance a lick.

How was she going to survive watching him for another five years? By keeping her fingers crossed and toughing up, that's how.

When all the congratulations were made and the pictures taken and the TV interviews done, he found her still sitting in the stands alone.

She threw her arms around him, feeling him solid beneath her touch. This man was worth every scary moment they'd share for the next hundred years.

"Ever think you'd be a millionaire?" Kade said, towering over her, all smiles.

She shook her head, the reality of the win and the money not sinking in yet. All she knew was Kade was safe. That was all she cared about.

"I've got next year all planned out. It will take some travel, but you'll love it."

She doubted that, but kept her opinion to herself. Watching Kade ride week after week was going to give her a heart attack. She pasted on a smile. "Okay. What have you come up with?"

"We have a couple of months off, so I thought we could travel to Montana and see my folks, and yours if you want." He sank down her, propping his boots on the seat in front of them. He handed her a half empty bottle of Bud.

"I'd like to see your parents." She took a swallow of the beer, the cool liquid washing down the lump in her throat. "But I think I'll wait a while before I talk to mine. Then what?"

"Well, that's the thing. I probably should have asked you first, but I'm hanging up my bull rope."

"Say that again." Although he didn't seem drunk, Kade must have had way more than this one beer.

"Now I know you're set on traveling to a bunch of bull ridings with the new TBC World Champion, and I hate to burst your bubble." He wrapped his arm around her shoulders and pulled her close, planting a soft kiss on the top of her head. "But I'm retiring. I never did think a guy should overstay his welcome. Better to go out on top, don't you think?"

His words were perfectly normal, words she'd longed to hear, but her brain couldn't process what he said. "So no more bulls? Are you okay with that?"

Kade stood, keeping his steely gray eyes trained on hers.

As she watched, he dropped to one knee.

"I'm more than good with this." Leaning forward, he gave Pansy a toe-curling kiss. "Besides, I'll have too much to do to keep traveling the circuit. I have a business to run, a ranch to buy and a woman to love for the rest of my life."

Romance Beneath A Rodeo Moon

If you enjoyed reading Sweet Cowboy Kisses, you can find Cary and Micah's story in *Gimme Some Sugar*, the first in the Sugar Coated Cowboys series.

Gimme Some Sugar-Pastry chef, Cary Crockett, is on the run. Pursued by a loan shark bent on retrieving gambling debts owed him by her deadbeat ex-boyfriend, she finds the perfect hiding place at the remote Circle W Ranch. More at home with city life, cupcakes and croissants than beef, beans and bacon, she has to convince ranch owner Micah West she's up to the job of feeding his hired hands. The overwhelming attraction she feels toward him was nowhere in the job description.

Micah West has a big problem. The camp-cook on his central Oregon ranch has up and quit without notice, and his crew of hungry cowboys is about to mutiny. He agrees to hire Cary on a temporary basis, just until he finds the right man to fill the job. Maintaining a hands-off policy toward his sexy new cook becomes tougher than managing a herd of disgruntled wranglers. http://amzn.to/1UDCemK

More books by Stephanie Berget featuring rodeo cowboys, ranchers and the women who love them:

Radio Rose-Cowboys and aliens … on a dark, deserted highway, it can be hard to tell the difference.

Especially when Rose Wajnowski makes her living as a night DJ chatting about alien encounters with folks in tinfoil helmets. Her listeners are eccentric, to say the least. But she's happy—sort of—with her solitary life. Until a midnight car crash and a blow to the head has her seeing tall, handsome extra-terrestrials instead of stars.

Adam Cameron, raised by his narcissistic grandfather, got out of Tullyville, Colorado the day he turned eighteen. He's back ten years later for the reading of his grandfather's will, but he's not happy to be home. Except for meeting the pretty little brunette who nearly ran him down with her car on that dark highway.

Adam is about to be pulled into a contest for a vast fortune and the future of a town he'd just as soon forget. But the quirky inhabitants of Tullyville desperately need his help if their town is to survive. Luckily for him, this cowboy has feisty Rose at his side, and in his arms.

As they work together to save their town, Rose and Adam learn important lessons about trust and the real meaning of family. http://amzn.to/267wmd6

Sugarwater Ranch-Sean O'Connell's life is perfect, or it was until his partying lifestyle affected his bull riding. Now he's ended the season too broke to leave the Northwest for the warm southern rodeos. When a wild night with his buddies gets out of hand, he wakes up naked, staring into the angry eyes of a strange woman. His infallible O'Connell charm gets him nowhere with the dark-haired beauty. It's obvious she's not his usual good-time girl, so why can't he forget her?

Bar-manager Catherine Silvera finds a waterlogged, unconscious cowboy freezing to death in front of the Sugarwater Bar. She saves his life--then runs faster than a jackrabbit with a coyote on its tail. Any man who makes his living rodeoing is bad news, especially if he thinks partying is part of the competition. He's everything she doesn't want in a man, so why can't she shake her attraction to the rugged cowboy?
http://amzn.to/29lydml

Changing A Cowboy's Tune: Rodeo Road series, book 1. When her fiancé demands Mavis abandon her goal of barrel racing at the National Finals Rodeo, she chooses to follow her dream and loses the man she adores.

Dex wants nothing more than to marry the woman he loves and build a future on his family's ranch, but when he pushes her to settle into life as a mother and rancher's wife, she bolts. Years apart haven't dampened their desire, but can they see past their own dreams for the future and invent a life they both love?

https://www.amazon.com/Changing-Cowboys-Tune-Rodeo-

Road/dp/1546814892/ref=asap_bc?ie=UTF8

Gimme Some Sugar Excerpt

Snapping his head up, he whirled around, almost elbowing the woman standing behind him. Pulling in a deep, slow breath, partly to gather some semblance of calm and partly to adjust to the tingle where her hand met his arm, he took a step back before speaking.

"Help me with what?" Did he know her? He was sure he didn't, but man….

"I'm sorry. I didn't mean to eavesdrop, but I heard you say you're looking for a cook." Golden eyes the color of whiskey stared into his. "I cook."

He let his gaze wander over her, liking what he saw. She wasn't a local. Her white blond hair was as short as a man's on the sides and curled longer on the top and back. He hadn't seen any woman, or anyone at all who wore their hair like this. Of course, tastes of the people of East Hope ran to the conservative.

Despite the severe hairstyle, she was pretty. Beyond pretty. Leather pants showed off her soft curves, miniature combat boots encased her small feet and a tight tank top enhanced her breasts.

When she cleared her throat, he jerked his eyes up to her face. "It won't do you any good to talk to my breasts. Like most women, it's my brain that answers questions."

A smart ass and she'd caught him red-handed. His cheeks warmed. Damn it, he was blushing. This woman was not at all what he needed. Time to end this. "I have a ranch, the Circle W. We need a camp cook. A man."

Her eyes narrowed, and her body tensed. "It looks like you need any kind of cook you can get." She held her hand out, indicating the empty café. "Not a lot of takers."

She had him there. His gut told him he was going to regret this, but she was right. He had no choice. "I'll hire you week to week." When she nodded, he continued. "I've got seven ranch hands. You'll cook breakfast and dinner and pack lunches, Monday through Friday and serve

Sunday dinner to the hands who are back by six o'clock."

She bounced on the toes of her feet until she noticed him watching her then she pulled on a cloak of calm indifference. "You won't regret this."

He felt a smile touch the corners of his mouth as his gut twisted. "I already do."

http://amzn.to/1UDCemK

ABOUT THE AUTHOR

Stephanie Berget was born loving horses and found her way to rodeo when she married her own, hot cowboy. She and her husband traveled throughout the Northwest while she ran barrels and her cowboy rode bucking horses. She started writing to put a realistic view of rodeo and ranching into western romance. Stephanie and her husband live on a farm, located along the Oregon/Idaho border. They raise hay, horses and cattle, with the help of Dizzy Dottie, the Border Collie and Cisco, team roping horse extraordinaire.

Stephanie is delighted to hear from readers. Reach her at http://www.stephanieberget.com
Facebook:
https://www.facebook.com/stephaniebergetwrites/
Twitter: https://twitter.com/StephanieBerget